Stephen Harriman Long

Voyage in a Six-Oared Skiff

to the falls of Saint Anthony in 1817

Stephen Harriman Long

Voyage in a Six-Oared Skiff
to the falls of Saint Anthony in 1817

ISBN/EAN: 9783337336028

Printed in Europe, USA, Canada, Australia, Japan

Cover: Foto ©Andreas Hilbeck / pixelio.de

More available books at **www.hansebooks.com**

VOYAGE

IN A

SIX-OARED SKIFF

TO THE

FALLS OF SAINT ANTHONY

IN 1817.

BY

MAJOR STEPHEN H. LONG,

TOPOGRAPHICAL ENGINEER UNITED STATES ARMY.

WITH INTRODUCTORY NOTE

BY

EDWARD D. NEILL,

SECRETARY MINNESOTA HISTORICAL SOCIETY.

PHILADELPHIA:

HENRY B. ASHMEAD, BOOK AND JOB PRINTER,

Nos. 1102 AND 1104 SANSOM STREET.

1860.

INTRODUCTORY NOTE.

This Journal, for the first time published, was written by STEPHEN H. LONG, now a veteran and honored Colonel of the Corps of Topographical Engineers of the United States Army.

The voyage was performed in a six-oared skiff, presented to Major Long by Governor William Clark, the Superintendent of Indian Affairs at Saint Louis. Having returned from a tour to the portage of the Fox and Wisconsin Rivers, he ascended from Prairie du Chien to the Falls of Saint Anthony.

The objects of his voyage were to meander and sketch the course of the Upper Mississippi, to exhibit the general topography of the shores, and to designate such sites as were suitable for military purposes.

The manuscript was placed in the hands of Keating in 1823, who frequently refers to it in his History of the Expedition to the Sources of the St. Peter, now Minnesota River.

Written nearly a half century ago, containing the first account of the legends of Maiden Rock and the Falls of Saint Anthony, and describing the actual appearance of Indian villages then on the sites of numerous busy towns of the present day, it must ever be perused with interest, and considered an important contribution to the Historical Collections of Minnesota.

The writer cannot omit the expression of indebtedness to the venerable author, and also to Dr. Edwin James, of Burlington, Iowa, for the courtesy manifested in granting the manuscript for publication.

E. D. N.

St. Paul, Minnesota.

JOURNAL.

Wednesday, July 9.—Learning that there was little or
no danger to be apprehended from the Indians living on
the Mississippi above Prairie du Chien, I concluded to
ascend for the purpose of reconnoitering further up the
river. Layed in provision for sixteen days, and set
sail at half past eight this morning with a favorable
wind. I took an additional soldier on board at the
Fort, so that my crew now consisted of seven men. My
former interpreter not being acquainted with the language
of the Indians living on this part of the river, I had occasion to dismiss him and employ another. The name of my
present interpreter is Rock or Roque, whose father was a
Frenchman and mother a squaw of the Sioux nation.
But as he was not acquainted with the English language,
nor I with the French sufficiently to converse with him,
I stood in need of some person to interpret his conver-
sation in English. A gentleman by the name of Hempstead, a resident of Prairie du Chien, having some desire
to ascend the Mississippi, had the politeness to volunteer
his services as French interpreter, and ascend the river
in company with me. The whole number on board of
my boat was now ten persons. Mr. Hempstead was a
native of New London, Connecticut, but has resided in
this part of the country about eight years.

There sailed also in company with us, two young
gentlemen from New York, by the name of King and
Gun, who are grandsons of Capt. J. Carver, the celebrated
traveler.   They had taken a bark canoe at Green Bay,
and were on their way to the northward, on a visit to
the Sauteurs, for the purpose of establishing their claims
to a tract of land granted by those Indians to their
grandfather.   They had waited at Prairie du Chien,
during my trip up the Ouisconsin, in order to ascend the
Mississippi with me.   On board their boat were three .
men beside themselves; so that our whole party consisted of fifteen persons.   Passed Yellow River on our
left, about two miles from the Fort.   It is navigable for
pirogues, in time of high water, about fifty miles from
its mouth.   About one mile further up is a creek of
considerable size coming in on the same side, called the
Painted Rock.   One and a half miles higher is a small
prairie on the east side, at the upper end of the Prairie
du Chien, called Prairie des Sioux, at which the Sioux
Indians are in the habit of stopping to dress and paint
themselves, when they are on their way to visit the
garrison below.   Passed a prominent part of the bluffs
on our left, called Cape Puant.   The circumstance from
which it derived its name was as follows.   The Sioux
and Puants were about to commence hostilities against
each other; and a large party of the latter set out on
an expedition, to invade the territory of the Sioux and
attack them by surprise.   But the Sioux gaining intelligence of their design assembled a superior force, and
laid in ambush, waiting for the Puants to land on this
side.   Immediately after their landing the Sioux rushed

down from the bluffs; attacked the Puants in a small recess, between two promontories, drove them into the river, and massacred the whole party. Just above this is Garlic Cape, remarkable from the singularity of its appearance. In shape it resembles a cone, cut by a perpendicular plane passing through its apex and base. Its height is about four hundred and fifty feet. A little east of its base is a fine spring. The valley of the river in this part is almost entirely occupied by the river, which spreads in some places to the width of three or four miles, giving place to numerous islands, some of which are very large. The bluffs are generally between four and five hundred feet high, cut with numerous ravines, and exhibiting other signs of being the commencement of a very hilly and broken inland country. The wind failed us about eleven A. M., and we had occasion to row the rest of the day. Encamped on the head of an island about sunset. Distance twenty-eight and a half miles.

Thursday, 10.—Our companions in the birch canoe encamped on the same island but about four miles below us. The weather calm this morning. Got under way at sunrise and came six miles before breakfast, during which we caught five catfish and one drum. A favorable wind then rising, we set sail. Passed a small recess on our right, formerly occupied by a party of Winnebagoes as a village. It now contains but two small wigwams, having been deserted by its former occupants in consequence of a disaster that befell one of their party. In time of the late war, Gov. Clark of St. Louis ascended the Mississippi for the purpose of establishing a military post at Prairie du Chien. On his arrival at that place he found there eight Indians who were inhabitants of this village, and made prisoners of them, as they had taken part with our enemies. They were confined in the house now occupied by Mr. Hempstead, and a guard set to keep them secure. Apprehending that they should be treated with severity, they were meditating a plan whereby to effect their escape; when one of their number hit upon an expedient which they afterwards adopted. His plan was for one of the party to break through a window and seize the sentinel, when there should happen to be but one on post, and hold him fast till the rest should make their escape. But aware that the one who should execute this part of the plot must expose himself to almost certain death, he offered to sacrifice himself for the safety of the others; and an opportunity presenting he leaped through the window, seized the sentinel, whose attempts to stab him with his bayonet he effectually frustrated, and held him fast till the rest had got out of danger. He then released the sentinel and attempted to make his escape but was immediately fired upon by the sentinel and received a wound in the knee, of which he died a short time after; although it did not prevent him from effecting his escape at the time.

Passed Little Ioway River coming in from the west. There is a small village of Foxes about three miles up this river, consisting of five or six wigwams. The river is navigable in time of high water about fifty miles, and at all times a little above the Indian village. Its current is generally rapid but not precipitate. Passed several

Sioux lodges or wigwams on our left, at which there was a small war party of ten or twelve Indians. As soon as they saw our flag they hoisted American colors, and we returned the compliment by discharging a blunderbuss, upon which they fired two guns ahead of us. Finding we were not disposed to call on them, (for we had a very fine wind), six of the young warriors, very fine looking fellows, took a canoe and waited on us. We slackened sail to enable them to overtake us. When they came up their chief warrior gave me his hand and a few common-place remarks passed between us. I gave him some tobacco and a pint of whisky, and they left us, apparently very well satisfied.

Passed Raccoon Creek, an inconsiderable stream coming in from the eastward. ·

Since we left Prairie du Chien, have not been able at any place to see both sides of the river at the same time, owing to the numerous islands which the river imbosoms. The bluffs generally make their appearance immediately upon the shore of the river, on both sides. They are intersected by numerous ravines which divide them into knobs and peaks towering four or five hundred feet above the level of the river. The rocky stratifications are almost exclusively sandstone, of a yellowish appearance, inclining to be soft and spongy, rather than brittle and crumbling. Numerous bluffs of a semi-conical form, resembling Cape Garlic before described, only in many instances are much larger, are arranged along the sides of the river. Their faces are perpendicular cliffs of the above mentioned sandstone. Passed the mouth of Root River on our left. It is navigable in high water about

forty or forty-five miles, and in low about twenty.   There
are no Indians living upon it at present, but hunting
parties frequently encamp in the neighborhood of it.
The wind very favorable most of the day.   Encamped
on the west side of the river, a little above the Root
River, at a late hour.   Distance fifty miles.

Friday, 11.—In the latter part of the night, a violent
storm from the north-east, accompanied with very heavy
thunder, commenced and continued till morning.   Got
under way at sunrise, the weather calm and cloudy.
Passed Prairie de la Cross on our right, upon which we
observed a small enclosure which was the burying place
of the son of an Indian chief.   Upon his grave a pole
was erected, to which an American flag was attached.
The flag was almost worn out, having been suspended
for a considerable time.   At the upper part of the prairie was a small encampment of Winnebagoes—the most
civil of any of that nation I have met with.   They gave
us a large number of turtles' eggs, of which they had
collected nearly half a bushel, and in return I gave them
some tobacco.   This party belongs to a small band of
Winnebagoes, living about six miles up the Prairie de la
Cross Creek, which comes in from the north-east at the
head of the Prairie.   The band consists of forty or fifty
men, besides women and children.

These Indians were peaceable during the late war, and
have always manifested a friendly disposition towards
the Americans.   Collected several specimens of curious,
though not very interesting, minerals; amongst which
were iron-ore, red sandstone, some parts of which were
of a vermilion hue, and sandstone of a yellowish cast,

containing abundance of extremely small shells, and other organic remains. Met three canoes of Sioux Indians. Passed the Black River on our right, coming in from the N. N. E. It is navigable for pirogues somewhat more than one hundred miles, to where the navigation is obstructed by rapids. On this river is an abundance of pine timber of an excellent quality. Much of the pine timber used at St. Louis is cut here. This river has three mouths, by which it discharges itself into the Mississippi, the lowermost of which is most passable, and communicates with the Mississippi twelve or fourteen miles below the junction of the valleys of the two rivers. The bluffs along the river to-day were unusually interesting. They were of an exceedingly wild and romantic character, being divided into numerous detached fragments, some of them of mountainous size, while others in slender conical peaks, seemed to tower aloft till their elevation rendered them invisible. Here might the poet or bard indulge his fancy in the wildest extravagance, while the philosopher would find a rich repast in examining the numerous phenomena here presented to his view, and in tracing the wonderful operations of nature that have taken place since the first formation of the world.

A little above the mouth of Black River, both shores of the Mississippi may be seen at the same time, which is the only instance of the kind we have met with on our way from Prairie du Chien to this place. One mile further ahead the bluffs on both sides approach within eight hundred yards of each other, and the river in consequence is narrower here than at any other place this side of Prairie du Chien. Notwithstanding this contraction of its channel, the river here imbosoms an island of considerable size. The wind hard ahead most of the day. Encamped about sunset on a small island. Distance twenty-six and a half miles.

Saturday, 12.—Within a few yards of the island where we encamped is another, considerably smaller, which, for the sake of brevity, I called the Bluff Islands, as its former name is very long and difficult to pronounce. It has been accounted a great curiosity by travelers. It is remarkable for being the third island of the Mississippi, from the Gulf of Mexico to this place, that has a rocky foundation similar to that of the neighboring bluffs, and nearly the same altitude. Pike, in his account of it, states the height of it to be about two hundred feet. We lay by this morning for the purpose of ascertaining its altitude, which we found by a trigonometrical calculation, which my instruments would not enable me to make with much accuracy, to be a little more than five hundred feet. It is a very handsome conical hill, but not sufficiently large to deserve the appellation of mountain, although it is called by the name of the Montaigne qui trompe de l'eau, or the mountain that is soaked in the water. When we stopped for breakfast, Mr. Hempstead and myself ascended a high peak to take a view of the country. It is known by the name of the Kettle Hill, having obtained this appellation from the circumstance of its having numerous piles of stone on its top, most of them fragments of the rocky stratifications which constitute the principal part of the hill, but some of them small piles made by the Indians. These at a distance have some similitude of kettles arranged along upon the ridge and sides of the hill. From this, or almost any other eminence in its neighborhood, the beauty and grandeur of the prospect would baffle the skill of the most ingenious pencil to depict, and that of the most accomplished pen to describe. Hills marshaled into a variety of agreeable shapes, some of them towering into lofty peaks, while others present broad summits embellished with contours and slopes in the most pleasing manner; champaigns and waving valleys; forests, lawns, and parks alternating with each other; the humble Mississippi meandering far below, and occasionally losing itself in numberless islands, give variety and beauty to the picture, while rugged cliffs and stupendous precipices here and there present themselves as if to add boldness and majesty to the scene. In the midst of this beautiful scenery is situated a village of the Sioux Indians, on an extensive lawn called the Aux Aisle Prairie; at which we lay by for a short time. On our arrival the Indians hoisted two American flags, and we returned the compliment by discharging our blunderbuss and pistols. They then fired several guns ahead of us by way of a salute, after which we landed and were received with much friendship. The name of their chief is Wauppaushaw, or the Leaf, commonly called by a name of the same import in French, La Feuille, or La Fye, as it is pronounced in English. He is considered one of the most honest and honorable of any of the Indians, and endeavors to inculcate into the minds of his people the sentiments and principles adopted by himself. He was not at home at the time I called, and I had no opportunity of seeing him. The Indians, as I suppose, with the expectation

2

that I had something to communicate to them, assembled themselves at the place where I landed and seated themselves upon the grass. I inquired if their chief was at home, and was answered in the negative. I then told them I should be very glad to see him, but as he was absent I would call on him again in a few days when I should return. I further told them that our father, the new President, wished to obtain some more information relative to his red children, and that I was on a tour to acquire any intelligence he might stand in need of. With this they appeared well satisfied, and permitted Mr. Hempstead and myself to go through their village. While I was in the wigwam, one of the subordinate chiefs, whose name was Wazzecoota, or Shooter from the Pine Tree, volunteered to accompany me up the river. I accepted of his services, and he was ready to attend me on the tour in a very short time. When we hove in sight the Indians were engaged in a ceremony called the *Bear Dance;* a ceremony which they are in the habit of performing when any young man is desirous of bringing himself into particular notice, and is considered a kind of initiation into the state of manhood. I went on to the ground where they had their performances, which were ended sooner than usual on account of our arrival. There was a kind of flag made of fawn skin dressed with the hair on, suspended on a pole. Upon the flesh side of it were drawn certain rude figures indicative of the dream which it is necessary the young man should have dreamed, before he can be considered a proper candidate for this kind of initiation; with this a pipe was suspended by way of sacrifice. Two arrows were stuck up at the foot of the pole, and fragments of painted feathers, etc., were strewed about the ground near to it. These pertained to the religious rites attending the ceremony, which consist in bewailing and self-mortification, that the Good Spirit may be induced to pity them, and succour their undertaking.

At the distance of two or three hundred yards from the flag, is an excavation which they call the bear's hole, prepared for the occasion. It is about two feet deep, and has two ditches, about one foot deep, leading across it at right angles. The young hero of the farce places himself in this hole, to be hunted by the rest of the young men, all of whom on this occasion are dressed in their best attire and painted in their neatest style. The hunters approach the hole in the direction of one of the ditches, and discharge their guns, which were previously loaded for the purpose with blank cartridges, at the one who acts the part of the bear; whereupon he leaps from his den, having a hoop in each hand, and a wooden lance, the hoops serving as forefeet to aid him in characterizing his part, and his lance to defend him from his assailants. Thus accoutered he dances round the place, exhibiting various feats of activity, while the other Indians pursue him and endeavor to trap him as he attempts to return to his den, to effect which he is privileged to use any violence he pleases with impunity against his assailants, and even to taking the life of any of them.

This part of the ceremony is performed three times, that the bear may escape from his den and return to it again through three of the avenues communicating with it. On being hunted from the fourth or last avenue, the bear must make his escape through all his pursuers if possible, and flee to the woods, where he is to remain through the day. This, however, is seldom or never accomplished, as all the young men exert themselves to the utmost in order to trap him. When caught he must retire to a lodge erected for his reception in the field, where he is to be secluded from all society through the day, except one of his particular friends whom he is allowed to take with him as an attendant. Here he smokes and performs various other rites which superstition has led the Indians to believe are sacred. After this ceremony is ended the young Indian is considered qualified to act any part as an efficient member of their community. The Indian who has had the good fortune· to catch the bear and overcome him when endeavoring to make his escape to the woods, is considered a candidate for preferment, and is on the first suitable occasion appointed the leader of a small war party in order that he may further have an ·opportunity to test his prowess and perform more essential service in behalf of his nation. It is accordingly expected that he will kill some of their enemies and return with their scalps. I regretted very much that I had missed the opportunity of witnessing this ceremony, which is never performed except when prompted by the particular dreams of one or other of the young men, who is never complimented twice in the same manner on account of his dreams.

Passed several places where the prospect was very agreeable. The winds strong ahead all day. Encamped on a sand-bar. Distance twenty-one miles.

Sunday, 13—Caught several fish last night. The

atmosphere loaded with vapor this morning; the mercury
at 51°. Started at sunrise but had to lay by on account
of the fog. A favorable breeze sprung up from the S. E.
about eight and we hoisted sail. Saw a numerous flock
of pelicans. They flew up from a sand-bar a little before
us, and continued sailing about us for some time, which
is usual with them, till they arose to a very great height
when they disappeared. Passed Embarrass River on
our left coming in from the west. Just above its confluence with the Mississippi it unites its waters with Clear
Water Creek. The former is navigable in high water
thirty or forty miles, the latter about fifteen miles. The
Indians frequently hunt in the neighborhood of these
rivers, but have no permanent establishment upon them.
A little above this our Indian companion informed us
that he was fired upon seven times by a party of Chippeways but received no injury. He was alone and
unarmed at the time, but the Chippeways fled immediately after firing upon him. Passed the cabin also
where my interpreter spent the last winter in trading
with the Indians—at present unoccupied. Met the
nephew of La Feuille, and another Indian, who were on
a hunting expedition. My interpreter informed the
nephew who is to succeed his uncle in the office of chief,
that a party of the Sioux Indians of his village had
followed us, to beg whisky, after we had given them
all we thought it prudent to part with. He appeared
much offended that they should have done so, and eagerly
inquired if his uncle was not at home to restrain them.
We gave them some tobacco and whisky and left them.
Were much amused by the singing of our chief, who felt

a disposition to be merry after taking whisky. He appears to be a man of veracity, firmness, and bravery. He occasionally stands up in the boat and harangues with a loud voice, proclaiming who he is, where he is going, and the company he is with. Passed the River au Bœuf coming in from the north. It is of moderate size and is navigable in high water about thirty miles. Buffaloes are found on this river which gives occasion to its name; the Indians hunt them here in all seasons; they are not however very numerous. Opposite to the mouth of this river, on the west side of the Mississippi, is a large prairie, situated between the bluffs and the river, being about two miles in width; on a part of it is a scattering growth of timber. Should there be occasion to send troops into this quarter, they might be posted to advantage at this place, as the position would be secure, and at the same time, afford a tolerable command of the river. The elevation of the prairie above the river is about twenty-five feet. Upon the upper end of the prairie is the Grand Encampment, or place of general resort for the Indian traders, during the winter, for the purpose of trafficking with the Indians.

Arrived at the foot of Lake Pepin about dark. The wind favorable, but very gentle, through the day. Distance thirty-five miles.

Monday, 14.—The wind blew violently from the S. E. through the night, but as it was too dark to take our courses, we could not avail ourselves of the advantage it otherwise would have been to us. Set sail at an early hour, but the wind soon shifted into the N. W., and was so strong ahead that we could make but very little

progress either by rowing or cordelling. Were in consequence delayed about one and a half hours, during
which Mr. H. and myself ascended the bluff in order to
enjoy a prospect of the neighboring country. The place
where we were was at the lower extremity of Lake
Pepin. From the height we had a view, not only of the
lake and the majestic bluffs that bound it, but also of the
surrounding country to a considerable extent. The
contrast between this and the view we had two days
before is very striking. The bluffs are more regular and
more uniform in their height. The back country is
rolling rather than hilly, and has comparatively but
little timber upon it, particularly on the west of the
river. The valley between the bluffs which was before
thronged with islands, sand-bars, pools and marshes, is
here occupied by a beautiful expanse of water with
nothing to obstruct the view upon its surface, but the
shores of the lake. At the lower end of Lake Pepin
which has its general course about E. S. E. is Chippeway River coming in from the north. It is about five
hundred yards wide at its mouth, and is navigable for
pirogues about fifty miles at all times and in high water
much farther. From its appearance, however, I should
judge that its navigation must be much obstructed by
sand-bars. After breakfast we passed up the lake about
two miles, and stopped [on] the east shore for the
purpose of ascertaining the width of the lake and the
height of the bluffs where the high lands commence.
We found the lake a few yards short of two miles wide,
and the elevation of the hills four hundred and seventy-
five feet above the surface of the lake. About midway of

the lake passed the Lover's Leap, a prominent part of
the bluffs, with a perpendicular precipice of about one
hundred and fifty feet, and an abrupt descent of nearly
three hundred feet from its base to the waters edge.
At this place an unfortunate squaw met with an untimely
fate, as the consequence of her parents' obstinacy and
persecution.   The circumstances that led to this result
were related by our Indian chief and were the following.
Since his remembrance, a large party of the Sioux
Indians of La Feuille's band were going on a visit from
the river St. Peter's to Prairie du Chien.   When they
arrived at the hill now called the Lover's Leap, they
stopped to gather blue clay, which is found near the foot
of the hill, for the purpose of painting themselves.   Of .
this party was the young squaw who is the subject of
the story.   She had for a long time received the
addresses of a young hunter, who had formed an unconquerable attachment to her, and for whom she
entertained the strongest affection.   Her parents and
brothers were strenuously opposed to her choice, and
warmly seconded the solicitations of a young warrior who
was very much beloved by the nation for his bravery and
other good qualities.   To obviate her objections to the
warrior as being destitute of the means of clothing and
feeding her in consequence of the life he must lead in
order to perform the duties of his profession, her brothers
were at the expense of procuring everything that was
necessary to the ease and comfort of a family, and
presented them to the young warrior.   This they did
on the day of their arrival at the fatal spot, with the
hope that their sister would readily be prevailed upon to

marry the young man when all her objections to him
were thus obviated. She still persisted, however, in the
determination never to marry any but the object of her
sincere affection, the young hunter; while her parents
and brothers finding they could not accomplish their
purpose by gentle means, began to treat her with
severity. They insisted on her compliance with their
wishes, still summoning the arguments of filial duty and
affection in aid of their cause. She replied, "She did
not love the soldier and would live single forever rather
than marry him. You call me daughter and sister, as if
this should induce me to marry the man of your choice
and not of my own. You say you love me, yet you
have driven the only man that can make me happy far
from me. He loved me; but you would not let us be
happy together. He has therefore left me,—he has left
his parents and all his friends, and gone to bewail in the
woods. He cannot partake of the pleasure of this party.
He can do nothing but mourn. You are not satisfied with
all this. You have not made me miserable enough.
You would now compel me to marry a man I do not
love. Since this is your purpose, let it be so. You will
soon have no daughter or sister to torment, or beguile
with your false professions of love." The same day was
fixed upon as the day of her marriage with the warrior,
and the Indians were busily occupied in gathering clay
and painting themselves, preparatory for the nuptial
ceremony. She, in the meantime, walked aside from
the rest of the party, ascended to the top of the hill,
and called aloud to her parents and brothers, upbraiding
them for their unkind treatment. "You first refused to

let me marry agreeably to my own choice. You then
endeavored by artifice to unite me to a man I cannot
love, and now you will force me to marry him whether
I will or not. You thought to allure and make me
wretched, but you shall be disappointed." Her parents,
aware of her design, ran to the foot of the hill, and
entreated her to desist, with all the tenderness and
concern that parental fondness could suggest, rending
their hair and bewailing in the bitterest manner; while
her brothers attempted to gain the summit before she
should execute her fatal purpose. But all in vain; she
was determined and resolute. She commenced singing
her death song and immediately threw herself headlong
down the precipice, preferring certain and instantaneous
death, to a lingering state of unhappy wedlock.

Passed a large encampment of Sioux Indians, two
miles further up the lake, at which we left our chief.
As we hove in sight they hoisted the American flag,
which we saluted with a discharge of our blunderbuss.
Our salute was returned by the discharge of several guns
fired ahead of us. When we landed a crowd of Indians
came about us, and were very anxious that we should
stop a while with them. But the wind being strong and
favorable we concluded it best to make as little delay as
possible. We accordingly gave them some tobacco and
proceeded on. Lake Pepin is about twenty-one miles
long and of variable width from one and a half to three
miles. Through the greater part of its length it occupies
the whole width of the valley situated between the river
bluffs. There are however two prairies of considerable
size within the valley, that appear possessed of an excel-

lent soil, and are advantageously situated in regard to their elevation above the water. There are a few unimportant brooks emptying into the lake. About four miles above the lake is a river coming in from the west called Cannon river. Its navigation, etc. is similar to that of Root River before mentioned. It has a small band of Sioux Indians residing near its head. Passed an island a little above where two French traders were killed by an Indian a few years since. Encamped on a sand-bar at sunset. Wind favorable a part of the day. Distance thirty-five and a half miles.

Tuesday, 15.—Soon after we encamped last evening we received a visit from four Indians, two men and two boys; which gave me more satisfaction than any visit I had received from the Indians. They appeared very good humored and friendly. They asked for nothing. I gave them some tobacco and whisky for which they repeatedly thanked me. Gratitude is the noblest return that can be made for a kindness.

Set sail a half an hour before sunrise, with a favorable wind. Breakfasted a little below the place called the Crevasse, which is merely a fissure between two large rocks, affording a passage to a small stream of water. Ascending the bluff which is here no more than about one hundred and seventy five feet high, which is the common level of the country in this vicinity. Upon the slope of the bluffs observed a variety of pebbles and stones, amongst which were the agate of various hues, calcedony, flint, serpentine, ruby and rock crystal, etc. Pike in his journal describes the Mississippi for a considerable distance below the river St. Croix, as of a reddish appearance in shoal water, but black as ink in deep. The reddish appearance is occasioned by the sand at the bottom, which is of that complexion; the dark is no more than what is common to deep water moderately limpid. Met eight canoes of Indians headed by a trader whose name was the Elk's Head. They were merely on a hunting expedition, I gave the chief some tobacco. Passed the St. Croix River on our right. Its mouth is about one hundred yards wide, but immediately above it expands into a lake from three-quarters to two miles wide, and about thirty miles long. Throughout its whole extent it is deep and navigable for craft of very considerable burden. Its general course, from its head to its confluence with the Mississippi, is about S. E. About twenty miles above the lake in the river St. Croix are rapids by which the navigation of the river is entirely obstructed. Above the rapids the river is navigable for a considerable distance, in a direction towards Lake Superior. The water communication between Lake Superior and the Mississippi, is obstructed by a portage of moderate extent only, and is the channel of considerable intercourse between the British traders and the Indians. The Indians have no permanent villages either on the Lake, or the River St. Croix. They resort here annually, however, in large hunting parties, for wild game of almost all kinds, which is found here in great abundance. Gen. Pike on his expedition negotiated with the Indians for a tract of land comprehending the confluence of the St. Croix and Mississippi, and obtained a .grant of nine miles square. About four miles above the mouth of the St. Croix, as it is said, is the narrowest part of the Mississippi below the Falls of St. Anthony.   At this place we crossed the river from a dead start, with sixteen strokes of our oars.   The river is here probably between one hundred and one hundred and twenty yards wide, but as we had a favorable wind up the river we did not stop to measure it.   Upon supposition that the country, on ascending the Mississippi, would lose its alluvial and secondary character, after passing the Des Moin Rapids, and exhibit nothing but traits of primitive formations, not only in its precipices but even upon its surface, I had expected to find on this part of the river, not merely bluffs and knolls five or six hundred feet high, but, also, mountains of vast height and magnitude.   On the contrary I now discover that we have long since passed the highest lands of the Mississippi and that we are now moving through a rolling prairie country, where the eye is greeted with the view of extensive undulating plains, instead of being astonished by the wild gigantic scenery of a world of mountains.

The highlands on this part of the river are elevated from one to two hundred feet above the water level. The bluffs are more regular, both in their height and direction, than they are below Lake Pepin, and the valley of the river more uniform in its width.   The stratifications of the bluffs are almost entirely sandstone, containing clay and lime in greater or less proportions. The pebbles are a mixture of primitive and secondary stones of various kinds. Blue clay or chalk is frequently to be found.

Passed the Detour de Pin or Pine Turn of the Mississippi, which is the most westwardly bend of the river,

between St. Louis and the Falls of St. Anthony.   The
distance from this bend across to the River St. Peter's is
about nine miles, whereas it requires two days to go by
water to the same place on the St. Peter's.

The Mississippi above the St. Croix emphatically deserves the name it has acquired, which originally implies,
Clear River.   The water is entirely colorless and free
from everything that would render it impure, either to
the sight or taste.   It has a greenish appearance, occasioned by reflections from the bottom, but when taken
into a vessel is perfectly clear.

The wind was favorable through most of the day, but
the river in this part is very crooked, so that we could
not sail with so much expedition as otherwise we might
have done.   Encamped at sunset on the east side of the
river upon a handsome prairie. Distance forty-one miles.

Wednesday, 16.—Set sail at half past four this morning with a favorable breeze.   Passed an Indian burying
ground on our left, the first that I have seen surrounded
with a fence.   In the centre a pole is erected, at the
foot of which religious rites are performed at the burial
of an Indian, by the particular friends and relatives of
the deceased.   Upon the pole a flag is suspended when
any person of extraordinary merit, or one who is very
much beloved, is buried.   In the enclosure were two
scaffolds erected also, about six feet high and six feet
square.   Upon one of them were two coffins containing
dead bodies. ⎰Passed a Sioux village on our right containing fourteen cabins.   The name of the chief is the
Petit Corbeau, or Little Raven.   The Indians were all
absent on a hunting party up the River St. Croix, which

is but a little distance across the country from the village. Of this we were very glad, as this band are said to be the most notorious beggars of all the Sioux on the Mississippi. One of their cabins is furnished with loop holes, and is situated so near the water that the opposite side of the river is within musket-shot range from the building. By this means the Petit Corbeau is enabled to exercise a command over the passage of the river, and has in some instances compelled traders to land with their goods, and induced them, probably through fear of offending him, to bestow presents to a considerable amount, before he would suffer them to pass. The cabins are a kind of stockade buildings, and of a better appearance than any Indian dwellings I have before met with.

Two miles above the village, on the same side of the river, is Carver's Cave, at which we stopped to breakfast. However interesting it may have been, it does not possess that character in a very high degree at present. We descended it with lighted candles to its lower extremity. The entrance is very low and about eight feet broad, so that a man in order to enter it must be completely prostrate. The angle of descent within the cave is about 25°. The flooring is an inclined plane of quicksand, formed of the rock in which the cavern is formed. The distance from its entrance to its inner extremity is twenty-four paces, and the width in the broadest part about nine, and its greatest height about seven feet. In shape it resembles a baker's oven. The cavern was once probably much more extensive. My interpreter informed me that, since his remembrance, the entrance was not less than ten feet high and its length far greater than at present. The rock in which it is formed is a very white sandstone, so friable that the fragments of it will almost crumble to sand when taken into the hand. A few yards below the mouth of the cavern is a very copious spring of fine water issuing from the bottom of the cliff.

Five miles above this is the Fountain Cave, on the same side of the river, formed in the same kind of sandstone but of a more pure and fine quality. It is far more curious and interesting than the former. The entrance of the cave is a large winding hall about one hundred and fifty feet in length, fifteen feet in width, and from eight to sixteen feet in height; finely arched overhead, and nearly perpendicular. Next succeeds a narrow passage and difficult of entrance, which opens into a most beautiful circular room, finely arched above, and about forty feet in diameter. The cavern then continues a meandering course, expanding occasionally into small rooms of a circular form. We penetrated about one hundred and fifty yards, till our candles began to fail us, when we returned. To beautify and embellish the scene, a fine crystal stream flows through the cavern, and cheers the lonesome dark retreat with its enlivening murmurs. The temperature of the water in the cave was 46°, and that of the air 60°. Entering this cold retreat from an atmosphere of 89°, I thought it not prudent to remain in it long enough to take its several dimensions and meander its courses; particularly as we had to wade in water to our knees in many places in order to penetrate as far as we went. The fountain supplies an abundance of water as fine as I ever drank. This cavern, as I was informed by my interpreter, has been discovered but a few years. That the Indians formerly living in its neighborhood knew nothing of it till within six years past. That it is not the same as that described by Carver is evident, not only from this circumstance, but also from the circumstance that instead of a stagnant pool, and only one accessible room of a very different form, this cavern has a brook running through it, and at least four rooms in succession, one after the other. Carver's Cave is fast filling up with sand, so that no water is now to be found in it, whereas this, from the very nature of the place, must be enlarging, as the fountain will carry along with its current all the sand that falls into it from the roofs and sides of the cavern.

A little above we stopped to take a meridian altitude of the sun's lower limb, which we found to be 66° 42'.

Five miles above, the river St. Peter's comes in from the southwest. We arrived at the mouth of this river at 2 P. M., and layed by to dine. The St. Peter's is about two hundred yards wide at its mouth, and is navigable for Mackinaw boats between two and three hundred miles in all stages of the water; and in high water much further. For about forty miles it has still and deep water; farther up there are occasional rapids, by which there are portages of moderate extent. There are three considerable Indian villages up this river, the first of which is about nine miles above its mouth. They are all different bands of the Sioux nation. The country at the junction of the rivers I shall have occasion to describe on my return.

3

The rapids below the Falls of St. Anthony commence about two miles above the confluence of the Mississippi and St. Peter's, and are so strong that we could hardly ascend them by rowing, poleing, and sailing, with a strong wind, all at the same time. About four miles up the rapids we could make no headway by all these means, and were obliged to substitute the cordel in place of the poles and oars.

Arrived at the Falls of St. Anthony at a quarter past seven. Winds favorable a part of the day. Encamped on the east shore just below the cataract. Distance twenty-seven and a half miles.

Thursday, 17.—The place where we encamped last night needed no embellishments to render it romantic in the highest degree. The banks on both sides of the river are about one hundred feet high, decorated with trees and shrubbery of various kinds. The post oak, hickory, walnut, linden, sugar tree, white birch, and the American box; also various evergreens, such as the pine, cedar, juniper, etc., added their embellishments to the scene. Amongst the shrubbery were the prickly ash, plum, and cherry tree, the gooseberry, the black and red raspberry, the chokeberry, grape vine, etc. There were also various kinds of herbage and flowers, among which were the wild parsley, rue, spikenard, etc., red and white roses, morning glory, and various other handsome flowers. A few yards below us was a beautiful cascade of fine spring water, pouring down from a projecting precipice about one hundred feet high. On our left was the Mississippi hurrying through its channel with great velocity, and about three quarters of a mile above us, in plain view, was the majestic cataract of the Falls of St. Anthony. The murmuring of the cascade, the roaring of the river, and the thunder of the cataract, all contributed to render the scene the most interesting and magnificent of any I ever before witnessed.

The perpendicular fall of the water at the cataract, as stated by Pike in his journal, is sixteen and a half feet, which I found to be true by actual measurement. To this height, however, four or five feet may be added for the rapid descent which immediately succeeds the perpendicular fall within a few yards below. Immediately at the cataract the river is divided into two parts by an island which extends considerably above and below the cataract, and is about five hundred yards long. The channel on the right side of the Island is about three times the width of that on the left. The quantity of water passing through them is not, however, in the same proportion, as about one-third part of the whole passes through the left channel. In the broadest channel, just below the cataract, is a small island also, about fifty yards in length and thirty in breadth. Both of these islands contain the same kind of rocky formation as the banks of the river, and are nearly as high. Besides these, there are immediately at the foot of the cataract, two islands of very inconsiderable size, situated in the right channel also. The rapids commence several hundred yards above the cataract and continue about eight miles below. The fall of the water, beginning at the head of the rapids, and extending two hundred and sixty rods down the river to where the portage road commences, below the cataract is, according to Pike,

fifty-eight feet. If this estimate be correct the whole
fall from the head to the foot of the rapids, is not probably much less than one hundred feet. But as I had
no instrument sufficiently accurate to level, where the
view must necessarily be pretty extensive, I took no
pains to ascertain the extent of the fall. The mode I
adopted to ascertain the height of the cataract, was to
suspend a line and plummet from the table rock on the
south side of the river, which at the same time had very
little water passing over it as the river was unusually
low. The rocky formations at this place were arranged
in the following order, from the surface downward. A
coarse kind of limestone in thin strata containing considerable silex ; a kind of soft friable stone of a greenish
color and slaty fracture, probably containing lime, alumi-
num and silex; a very beautiful stratification of shell limestone, in thin plates, extremely regular in its formation
and containing a vast number of shells, all apparently of
the same kind. This formation constitutes the Table
Rock of the cataract. The next in order is a white or
yellowish sandstone, so easily crumbled that it deserves
the name of a sandbank rather than that of a rock. It
is of various depths, from ten to fifty or seventy-five feet,
and is of the same character with that found at the
caves before described. The next in order is a soft
friable sandstone, of a greenish color, similar to that
resting upon the shell limestone. These stratifications
occupied the whole space from the low water mark nearly
to the top of the bluffs. On the east, or rather north
side of the river, at the Falls, are high grounds, at the
distance of half a mile from the river, considerably more
elevated than the bluffs, and of a hilly aspect.

This remarkable part of the Mississippi, is not without a tale to hallow the scenery and add some weight to the interest it is naturally calculated to excite. Our Indian companion, the Shooter from the Pine Tree, related a story while he was with us, the catastrophe of which his mother witnessed with her own eyes.

A young Indian of the Sioux nation had espoused a wife with whom he had lived happily for a few years, enjoying every comfort of which a savage life is susceptible. To crown the felicity of the happy couple, they had been blessed with two lovely children, on whom they doated with the utmost affection. During this time the young man by dint of activity and perseverance, signalized himself in an eminent degree as a hunter, having met with unrivalled success in the chase. This circumstance contributed to raise him high in the estimation of his fellow savages, and draw a crowd of admirers about him, which operated as a spur to his ambition. At length some of his newly acquired friends desirous of forming a connection that must operate greatly to their advantage, suggested the propriety of his taking another wife, as it would be impossible for one woman to manage his household affairs and wait upon all the guests his rising importance would call to visit him. That his consequence to the nation was everywhere known and acknowledged, and that in all probability, he would soon be called upon to preside as their chief. His vanity was fired at the thought; he yielded an easy compliance with their solicitations, and accepted a wife they had already selected for him. After his second marriage it became an object with him, to take his new wife home, and reconcile his first wife to the match, which he was desirous of accomplishing in the most delicate manner, that circumstances would admit. For this purpose, he returned to his first wife, who was yet ignorant of what had taken place and by dissimulation attempted to beguile her into an approbation of the step he had taken. "You know," said he, "I can love no one so much as I love you; yet I see that our connection subjects you to hardships and fatigue, too great for you to endure. This grieves me much, but I know of only one remedy by which you can be relieved, and which, with your concurrence, shall be adopted. My friends from all parts of the nation, come to visit me, and my house is constantly thronged, by those who come to pay their respects, while you alone, are under the necessity of laboring hard in order to cook their food, and wait upon them. They are daily becoming more numerous and your duties instead of growing lighter, are becoming more arduous every day. You must be sensible that I am rising high in the esteem of the nation, and I have sufficient grounds to expect that I shall ere long be their chief. These considerations have induced me to take another wife, but my affection for you has so far prevailed over my inclination in this respect, as to lead me to solicit your approbation, before I adopt the measure. The wife I take shall be subject to your control in every respect, and will always be second to you in my affections." She listened to his narration with the utmost anxiety and concern, and endeavoured to reclaim him from his purpose, refuting all the reasons and pretences his duplicity had urged in favor of it, by unanswerable arguments, the suggestions of unaffected love and conjugal affection.

He left her however, to meditate upon the subject, in hopes that she would at length give over her objections and consent to his wishes. She in the mean time redoubled her industry, and treated him invariably with more marked tenderness, than she had done before, resolved to try every means in her power, to dissuade him from the execution of his purpose. She still however found him bent upon it. She plead all the endearments of their former life, the regard he had for the happiness of herself and the offspring of their mutual love, to prevail on him to relinquish the idea of taking another wife ; she warned him of the fatal consequences that would result to their family, upon his taking such a step. Till at length he was induced to communicate the event of his marriage. He then told her that a compliance on her part would be absolutely necessary. That if she could not receive his new wife as a friend and companion, she must admit her as a necessary incumbrance, at all events, they must live together. She was determined however, not to remain the passive dupe of his hypocrisy. She took her two children, left his house, and went to reside with her parents. Soon after her return to her father's family, she joined them and others of her friends in an expedition up the Missisippi, to spend the winter in hunting. In the spring as they were returning laden with peltries, she and her children occupied a canoe by themselves. On arriving near the Falls of St. Anthony, she lingered by the way, till the rest had all landed a little above the chute. She then painted herself and children, paddled her canoe immediately into the suck of the rapids, and commenced singing her death song, in which she recounted the happy scenes she had passed through when she enjoyed the undivided affection of her husband, and the wretchednes in which she was involved by his inconstancy.　Her friends alarmed at her situation, ran to the shore, and begged her to paddle out of the current; while her parents, in the agonies of despair, rending their clothes, and tearing out their hair, besought her to come to their arms.　But all to no purpose : her wretchedness was complete and must terminate only with her existence.　She continued her course till she was born headlong down the roaring cataract and instantly dashed to pieces on the rocks below.　No trace either of herself and children or the boat were ever found afterwards.　Her brothers to be avenged of the untimely fall of their sister, embraced the first opportunity and killed her husband, whom they considered the cause of her death.　A custom sanctioned by the usage of the Indians from time immemorial.

After having viewed the falls upon this side of the river, we attempted to cross the rapids in our boat, but the water was so low and the current so rapid, that we were compelled to return again to the same side, which we accomplished at the risk of having the boat wrecked upon a large rock, which we were but just able to shun. Made a second attempt, a little further down, in which we succeeded.　Having taken a view of the cataract on both sides, we commenced descending the river at a quarter past ten, A. M., in hopes that we should arrive at the mouth of the St. Peter's in time to take an observation for the latitude of that place.　But finding we were

likely to be pressed for time, we stopped one and a half
miles above, where we found the altitude of the sun's
lower limb, when on the meridian, to be 66°. After
arriving at the St. Peter's we lay by two or three hours,
in order to examine the country in that neighborhood.
At the mouth of this river is an island of considerable
extent, separated from the main by a slough of the Mississippi, into which the St. Peter's discharges itself.
Boats in ascending the former, particularly in low water,
usually pass through this slough, as it affords a greater
depth than the channel upon the other side of the island.
Immediately above the mouth of the St. Peter's is a
tract of flat prairie, extending far up this river and about
three hundred and fifty yards along the slough above
mentioned.   This tract is subject to inundation in time
of high water; which is also the case with the flat lands
generally, situated on both sides of these rivers.   Next
above this tract, is a high point of land, elevated about
one hundred and twenty feet above the water, and
fronting immediately on the Mississippi, but separated
from the St. Peter's by the tract above described.   The
point is formed by the bluffs of the two rivers intercept-
ing each other.   Passing up the river on the brow of the
Mississippi Bluff, the ground rises gradually for the
distance of about six hundred yards, when an extensive
broad valley of moderate depth commences.   But on the
St. Peter's the bluff retains nearly the same altitude,
being intersected occasionally by ravines of moderate
depth.   A military work of considerable magnitude
might be constructed on the point, and might be rendered
sufficiently secure by occupying the commanding height

in the rear in a suitable manner, as the latter would control not only the point, but all the neighboring heights, to the full extent of a twelve pounder's range. The work on the point would be necessary to control the navigation of the two rivers. But without the commanding work in the rear, would be liable to be greatly annoyed from a height situated directly opposite on the other side of the Mississippi, which is here no more than about two hundred and fifty yards wide. This latter height, however, would not be eligible for a permanent post, on account of the numerous ridges and ravines situated immediately in its rear.

Re-embarked and descended to the Fountain Cave, where we landed again and went into the cave for the purpose of taking some of its dimensions. Owing to the different states of the atmosphere, we could not penetrate so far by fifty yards as we did yesterday, before our candles went out. We measured the distance, as far as we went on this occasion, which we found to be one hundred and fifty yards. We embarked the third time, laid in a supply of wood for the night, kindled a fire in our cabouse, and concluded to float during the night. We regretted exceedingly that we could not spend more time in the enjoyment of the scenes we had been witnessing to-day, but were induced to forego the pleasure from the circumstance that our provisions were nearly exhausted, from a want of care in the destribution of them; that we had no whisky remaining, on the same account, which may be considered a necessary of life to those employed in the navigation of the Mississippi in hot weather. These concerns I had entrusted to my Corporal as it was impossible for me to manage them, and perform my other duties at the same time. But as he was appointed to officiate in that capacity at the commencement of the voyage, without ever having had the requisite experience before, he did not know how to distribute with proper economy, although he was extremely anxious to do so.

Friday, 18.—Floated all night, with no other inconvenience but occasionally running upon sand-bars. Landed at the River St. Croix for the purpose of examining the ground situated below the mouth of that river. At this place is a position well calculated for the command of both rivers; with the exception, that there is an island of the Mississippi, several miles long, situated opposite to the confluence of the two. On the west side of the Mississippi is a very small slough, that separates the island from the main land. This slough is navigable in high water, but its navigation may be effectually obstructed by constructing cheveux de frise and sinking them in the channel. With this exception a military post might be established here to considerable advantage, and would be sufficiently secure by occupying a commanding ground situated in rear of the site proposed, with an enclosed work constructed on the principle of the Martello Tower.

About twenty miles below the St. Croix met the grandsons of Carver before spoken of. We parted with them the second day after leaving Prairie du Chien, and saw nothing more of them till this day. We stopped a few minutes with them and gave them some instructions, to enable them to find the cave. We lay by a while at a Sioux village four and one-half miles above Lake Pepin in order to catch some fish, as we had nothing left of our provisions but flour. Our whisky also was all expended, and we had two hundred miles further to go before we could obtain a fresh supply. Caught three very fine catfish and killed a few pigeons. The village was kept in very nice order, exhibiting more signs of a well regulated police than any one I have met with on the voyage, with the exception of the Little Raven's before mentioned. The name of the chief of their village is Red Wing the elder. He and all his band were on a hunting tour at the time we were there. During our delay at this place Mr. H. and myself ascended a hill further down the river, called the Grange, or Barn, of which it has some faint resemblance. Its length is three-quarters of a mile and its height about four hundred feet. Its acclivity on the river side is precipitous, that on the opposite very abrupt. It is completely insulated from the other highlands in the neighborhood, which is also the case with many others, within a moderate distance, though not in quite so remarkable a manner; for this is not only surrounded by valleys, but is also nearly insulated by water, an arm or bay of the river entering at the lower end of the hill and extending within three or four hundred yards of the river above. Immediately upon the highest part of the Grange is one of the numerous artificial mounds that are to be met with in almost every part of this western world. Its elevation above its base however is only about five feet. I have observed that the mounds on the Mississippi, above the Illinois, though probably more numerous, are of a much smaller size, generally than those below, having been erected perhaps by a different nation of aborigines.

From the summit of the Grange the view of the surrounding scenery is surpassed, perhaps, by very few, if any, of a similar character that the country and probably the world can afford. The sublime and beautiful are here blended in most enchanting manner, while the prospect has very little to terrify or shock the imagination.

To aid in forming an idea approximating in some degree to the reality of the scene, we may suppose that the country at the head of Lake Pepin, situated between the main bluffs of the grand Mississippi Valley, has once been inundated to the height of two hundred and fifty feet above the present water level. That at this time the lake embosomed numerous small islands of a circular, oblong, and serpentine form. That from the main land also promontories and peninsulas projected into the lake on all sides, forming numerous capes, bays, and inlets. That the country bordering upon the lake was an extensive plain, in many places variegated with gentle hills and dales of the same general level with the islands and promontories. We may then suppose that by some tremendous convulsion that must have shaken the earth to its centre, this vast body of water has been drained off to its present humble level and left the bed of the lake free of water, and furnished with a rich and fertile alluvion, well adapted to vegetation of all kinds. That afterwards the valleys and knobs assumed a verdant dress, and those places which were once the haunts of the finny tribes now became the resorts of the feathered, and we shall have a faint idea of the outlines of the scene. But to be impressed with the sublimity, and delighted with the beauty of the picture, a view of the original is indispensable.

A favourable breeze springing up about dark, we concluded to set sail, as it was only four and a half miles to the lake, and after our arrival there we should sail without obstructions either of trees or sand bars.

Saturday, 19.—We had got into the broadest part of the lake about midnight, when the wind began to blow stronger, and there were at the same time strong indications of an approaching storm; we shifted our course and made for the shore as fast as possible, which we fortunately reached before the storm became violent. The night was so dark that we could find no harbor in which to secure our boat. We were engaged about one hour in towing her along the beach, in hopes of finding one, but the violence of the storm increased and the boat began to fill with water, so that we were forced to take out all our baggage with the least possible delay, all of which we had the good luck to save, without its having received much injury. We then made fast the boat and left her to fill, as it was out of our power to prevent her filling while the surf ran so high and strong. We succeeded in pitching our tent after much trouble, and got our baggage deposited within it. Our next object was to kindle a fire, but on inquiry found that our apparatus for that purpose was completely drenched in water. I then tore a piece of the lining from my coat sleeve, being the only place where I could find it dry, and kindled a fire with some dry rotten wood the men chanced to find

in the dark.' The day dawned soon after and we began
to make preparation for starting again, though the storm
continued with some abatement. We found that the
most important parts of our baggage had received but
little injury, and that our boat was not damaged. We
embarked again at half past six, rowed out into the lake
till we could clear a point lying a little to the leeward of
us, hoisted sail, and ran with great speed. The surf ran
so high and strong that we were in danger of filling
several times, as the waves broke over the sides of our
little bark. Called at the Indian village situated upon
Sandy Point, the same that we left our chief at, on our
outward voyage. He had promised to return with us,
but during our absence had been prevailed upon to join
the Indians of the village on a hunting expedition up
the Chippeway river, in which they were then about to
embark. The name of the chief of this village was Red
Wing, the younger, son of Red Wing spoken of yesterday. We delayed here but a very few minutes. Sailed
through the lake with a strong wind. At evening the
weather became calm, and we concluded to float through
the night. Lay by a short time about sunset to collect
wood and kindle a fire in our caboose, during which
caught three catfish.

Sunday, 20.—Met with no inconvenience in floating
except running foul of sand-bars occasionally, from which
we easily extricated ourselves. Passed Le Feuille, or
the Leaf's village, at which there were no Indians to be
seen, all of them having recently gone on a hunting cam-
paign. Stopped at the sand bar, where we took observations to ascertain the height of the Bluff Island, on

our passage up.   Here we found our axe which we lost
on that occasion.   Landed again on Bluff Island, for the
purpose of ascending to the top of the hill, which I did
in company with Mr. H.   Here we had a view of the
Indian village on Aux Ailes Prairie, as also of the beautiful scenery mentioned in my journal of Saturday, 12th
inst.   Here we discovered that what before appeared to
be the main river bluffs on the left, just below the
island, were a broken range of high bluff lands, towering
into precipices and peaks, completely insulated from the
main bluffs by a broad flat prairie.   This range, in
connection with the island, may be considered a great
curiosity, when we reflect that their sides have once
been buffeted by the billows of a lake, at least two
hundred feet above the present water level.   A little
below we saw three Indians on shore, engaged in killing
a rattlesnake.   They called to us and said that one of
their band had been bit on his leg by the snake, upon
which we waited for them to come to us.   Immediately
after the wound was inflicted they had cut out a piece
of the flesh containing the wounded part, and applied
bandages to the leg above.   I proposed salt and water
as a wash for the wound, but they objected, being
prejudiced against admitting water to a wound in any
case.   I had no sweet oil or anything else that I
thought serviceable, and could do nothing more but
advise them to return as soon as possible to their
encampment.

Layed by a while to ascend another hill, said to be
the highest on the Mississippi.   It is of a semi-conical
form as it presents itself to the view from the river, but

after ascending, it appears to be a ridge, the highest part of which projects towards the river, forming a high prominent peak, cleft perpendicularly from its summit about two hundred or two hundred and fifty feet. From this point it declines gradually till it loses itself in the bases of other hills farther from the river. The view from its summit direct to the river is rendered exceedingly terrific by one of the most frightful precipices I ever beheld. Even the largest trees below appear like stunted shrubbery, and the river seems to be almost inaccessible from its vast depression. I took observations for estimating the height of the hill, agreeably to which its elevation above the water is one thousand feet, but I am inclined to think some mistake was committed either in the measurement of the base line or in reading the angles from my sextant, as by the estimate the hill is much higher than I should judge it to be from its appearances. From this hill we also had a view of Bluff Island and its neighboring heights on the left shore, as well as the main bluffs of the river as far as the eye could reach. The beauty, grandeur, and magnificence of the scene, completely baffles description. The most curious and wonderful part of the scenery was the passage of the river between the main bluffs on the right and the insulated range before mentioned, on the left of the river. Here the river, not contented as in other places to meander through a valley several miles in width, seems to have left its original channel, preferring to cut a passage, just wide enough for its accommodation, through a cape or promontory six or eight hundred feet high, rather than embellish an extensive and beautiful lawn with its

4

peaceful waters. This phenomenon can be accounted for on no other principle, than the existence of a lake that once occupied the valley of the Mississippi, filling it to the height of many hundred feet above the present water level. This vast body of water may have given occasion to billows which wore upon the sandstone formations of the lake shores, and in process of time formed inlets, bays, peninsulas, and islands, so that when the water was drained off to its present level, the highlands and valley retained these singular conformations, as testimonials of the great damages they had experienced. On the top of the hill we collected many interesting specimens of minerals, such as crystals of iron ore, silicious crystalizations, beautifully tinged with iron, some of them purple, others reddish, yellow, white, etc., crusts of sandstone strongly cemented with iron, and I think set with solid crystals of quartz, etc. This hill would seem to be entitled to the appellation of mountain, were it not that the neighboring heights, and the highlands generally on this part of the river have very nearly the same altitude.

Monday, 21.—Floated last night also; had made very little progress on account of bad winds. While we stopped to breakfast, caught several fish, which, since we have no meat, are become essential to a healthy subsistence, particularly as my men have hard duty to perform.

Met twelve canoes of Fox Indians on a hunting tour from the Upper Ioway River. There were three very aged squaws with them, one of whom was entirely blind. She was busily engaged in twisting slips of bark for the purpose of making rush mats. This labor, notwithstanding her blindness and great age, she performed with much expedition.

Passed the Painted Rock on the right of the river, nine miles above Prairie du Chien. It has obtained this name from its having numerous hieroglyphics upon it, painted by the Indians. These figures are painted on a cliff nearly perpendicular, at the height of about twenty-five feet from its base. Whenever the Indians pass this cliff they are in the habit of performing certain ceremonies, which their superstition leads them to believe are efficacious in rendering any enterprise in which they may be engaged, successful.

Arrived at Prairie du Chien a little after nine o'clock in the evening, having accomplished the trip from this to the Falls of St. Anthony and back again, in thirteen days, being three days sooner than I had expected to return at the time of my departure from this place.

Tuesday, 22.—Found my friends at this place all very well excepting Captain Duffhey who had been bitten by a rattlesnake on the day of my departure. He received the wound in the instep where the tooth of the snake penetrated to the bone. He applied a bandage upon his leg in the first instance, and resorted to medical aid as soon as it was practicable. When he was bitten he was in the woods four miles from home, consequently the poison must have had a considerable time to diffuse itself, before he could apply a remedy. His foot and leg swelled very much and became black, but the remedies applied proved efficacious, and he is now past danger, and is so far recovered that he is able to walk about with ease.

Wednesday, 23.—Dr. Pearson, Lt. Armstrong and myself, took horses and rode about the neighborhood this morning, for the purpose of discovering a position better calculated for a military post, than the present site of Fort Crawford. We went down the Prairie to the Ouisconsin, then followed the course of that river about three miles above the commencement of the highlands, but could discover no position that was not objectionable in very many respects. The Prairie itself is separated from the Ouisconsin by a broad marshy tract of land, annually subject to inundation, which is the case also with some parts of the Prairie. The highlands are intersected by numerous ravines, and exhibit a constant succession of hills, ridges, and valleys of various depths. They are inaccessible from the river at many points, and overlook it at none, the view, as well as the command of the river, being effectually obstructed by the numerous islands which it imbosoms. Although there was no opportunity to accomplish the object of our reconnoitre, still, however, we had occasion to be highly gratified with a survey of curiosities that have baffled the ingenuity and penetration of the wisest to account for them. The curiosities alluded to are the remains of ancient works, constructed probably for military purposes, which we found more numerous and of greater extent upon the highlands, just above the mouth of the Ouisconsin, than any, of which a description has been made public, that have yet been discovered in the western country. They consist of ridges, or parapets of earth, and mounds, variously disposed so as to conform to the nature of the ground they are intended to fortify, the surface of which is variegated with numerous ridges, hills, valleys and ravines. The works of course have no regular form. The parapets are generally about three and a half feet high, with no appearance of a ditch upon either side, and are intercepted at short intervals by gateways or sallyports, most of which are flanked by parapets or mounds. The parapets are mostly situated upon ridges, some few, however, are disposed after the manner of traverses, being carried across the interior of the works in various directions. The mounds are from four to six feet in height, at present of a circular form, though square probably when first constructed. They are arrranged, in a straight direction, are about twenty feet asunder, and form continuation of the fortified lines, having the same direction as the parapets. Wherever there is an angle in the principal lines, a mound of the largest size is erected : the parapets also are generally terminated by mounds of this description, at the extremities of lines as also at the gateways. In many places the lines are composed of parapets and mounds in conjunction, the mounds being arranged along the parapet at their usual distance from each other and operating as flank defences to the lines. These works exhibit abundant evidence of having been erected at the expense of a vast deal of labor. Works of a similar character are to be found scattered through this part of the country in various directions. At what period they were constructed, and by what race of people, must in all probability forever remain a desideratum.

Thursday, 24.—Capt. Duffhey, Lt. Armstrong, Mr. Hempstead and myself took an excursion into the neigh-

boring high lands to-day, in order to ascertain, in some
measure, of what character they are, and to visit some
of the remains of ancient fortifications. We rode across
the country about twenty miles to Kickapoo Creek, and
returned again in a course different from that in which
we travelled out. The country is divided into numerous
hills, or rather ridges, of various shapes and dimensions,
but generally of an equal altitude ; by valleys and ravines,
some of which have fine streams of spring water running
through them. The hills are generally elevated from
three to four or five hundred feet above the valleys ;
handsomely rounded upon their tops, but abrupt and
precipitous on their sides, and almost inaccessible except
through the numerous ravines by which they are cut.
The valleys are many of them broad, and appear well
adapted to tillage and pasture. The highlands also
appear well calculated for the raising of grain. The
country is generally prairie land, but the hills and valleys
are in some places covered with a scattering growth of
fine timber, consisting of white, red, and post oak,
hickory, white walnut, sugar tree, maple, white and
blue ash, American box, etc. The antiquities were of
a similar character with those described yesterday. Of
these we saw numerous examples upon the hills and
ridges, as also a few in the valleys. Those on the ridges,
had the appearance of being designed to resist an attack,
on both sides, being for the most part a single parapet,
of considerable extent, crossed at right angles by traverses
at the distances of twenty or thirty yards from each
other, and having no ditch upon either side. Those in
the valleys appeared to have been constructed to com-

mand the passage of the particular valley in which they were situated. Some appeared as if they had been intended to defend against the attack of cavalry, as they were constructed across the heads of ravines through which horses must 'pass in order to get upon the top of the hills. We saw no works that exhibited signs of having been completed enclosures, but the whole were in detached parts, consisting of parapets, traverses, and mounds, forming lines and flanks.

We had designed also to visit a natural curiosity upon [the] banks of the same creek, but were not able to find it. Agreeably to the representations of several Indians whom I consulted on the occasion, it is a gigantic figure of stone resembling the human shape. It stands erect in a niche or recess formed in a precipice, the brow of which projects forward so as to overhang the figure. There are prominent parts of the precipice also, upon either side of the figure, resembling the jambs of a fire-place. The Indians pay religious homage to this figure, sacrificing tobacco, and other things they deem valuable, at the foot of it. The history they give of it, is, that a long time since a very bloody battle was fought at Prairie du Chien, in which vast numbers were slain, and the inhabitants of the Prairie vanquished. That a very good woman, after having received several wounds, made her escape from the carnage, and fled to the neighbouring hills, where she was like to famish for want of provisions. That the Good Spirit, pitying her condition, converted her into this monument of veneration and for a long time killed every Indian that dared approach in sight of it. But at length being tired of this havoc, he stayed his hand, and now suffers them to approach and worship it with impunity.

Friday, 25.—Spent the day in measuring and planning Fort Crawford and its buildings. The work is a square of three hundred and forty feet upon each side; and is constructed entirely of wood, as are all its buildings, except the magazine, which is of stone. It will accommodate five companies of soldiers. The enclosure is formed principally by the quarters and other buildings of the garrison, so that the amount of all the palisade work does not exceed three hundred and fifty feet in extent. The faces of the work are flanked by two block houses, one of which is situated in the S. E. and the other in the N. W. corner of the Fort, being alternate or opposite angles. The block houses are two stories high, with cupolas or turrets upon their tops. The first stories are calculated as flank defences to the garrison; the second afford an oblique flank defence, and at the same time guard the approach to the angles in which the block houses are situated, being placed diagonally upon the first. The turrets are fortified with oak plank upon their sides, and furnished with loop holes for muskets or wall pieces. The quarters, store-houses, etc., are ranged along the sides of the garrison, their rear walls constituting the faces of the work, which are furnished with loop holes at the distance of six feet from each other. The buildings are constructed with shed roofs, sloping inwards, so that their outward walls are raised twenty feet from the ground, thus presenting an insurmountable barrier to an assailing enemy; the buildings are all rough shingled, except the block houses which are covered with smooth shingles. The rooms are generally about nineteen feet square, most of them floored with oak plank, and all that were designed for quarters furnished with a door and window each in front. The magazine is twenty-four by twelve feet in the clear, the walls four feet thick, and the arch above supported by a strong flooring of timber. It has at present no other covering but the arch; preparations are making however to erect a roof over it, and cover it with shingles. The works are for the most part constructed of square timber, and the crevices in the walls of the buildings plastered with lime mortar, in such a manner as renders them comfortable habitations, except that the roofs are not well calculated to shed rain. The troops, however, are at present busily occupied in dressing shingles, cutting timber etc., in order to repair the defective parts of the works, and make additions where they are found necessary. Piazzas are to be built in front of all the quarters, floors to be laid, ceiling, etc., to be made, all of which are necessary to cleanliness and a well regulated police within the garrison. The building of these works was commenced on the 3d of July, 1816, by the troops stationed here under the command of Colonel Hamilton; previous to which no timber had been cut or stones quarried for the purpose. These articles were to be procured at the distance of from two to five miles from the site of the garrison, and transported to it in boats. The country where they were to be procured was so broken and hilly, that teams could not be employed even to convey them to the boats, but all must be done by manual labor. With all these disadvantages and hardships, and still

more, with a corrupt and sickly atmosphere, have the
soldiery at this place had to contend, in order to con-
struct works of sufficient magnitude and strength to
guard this part of our frontier.   A considerable part of
the work was done in the winter season, when at the
same time they were compelled to get their fuel at the
distance of two or three miles from the garrison, and in
many instances to draw it home by hand.   Yet no extra
compensation, either in pay or clothing, has been allowed
them in a single instance, although the whole of this
labor was unquestionably extra duty.

In regard to the eligibility of the site upon which
Fort Crawford is situated, very little can be said in favor,
but much against it.   Its relation to other parts of the
country would seem to give it a high claim to considera-
tion as a military post ; as also its central situation with
respect to our Indian neighbors.   But the disadvantages
under which works of moderate expense particularly
must lie, in this neighborhood, are too numerous to admit a doubt of the impropriety of placing confidence in
works of a similar character with those now constructed
while in a state of war.   The first objection that presents itself, is, that the situation, from the nature of the
place, must be unhealthy.   It is almost surrounded with
stagnant water at a short distance from the fort.   The
country about it abounds in marshes and low lands, annually subject to be overflowed, and the part of the
river lying immediately in front of the place, is very
little better than a stagnant pool, as its current is hardly
perceptible in low water.   In a military point of view
the objections to the present site, as also to any other

that might be fixed upon in the neighborhood, are various, and cannot easily be obviated. No complete command of the river can be had here, on account of the islands which it imbosoms. Directly opposite to the fort, and at the distance of six hundred and fifty yards from it, is an island two and a half miles in length, and seven hundred yards in breadth, separated from the east shore by a channel five hundred yards wide, and from the west by a channel two hundred and fifty yards. Both above and below this are numerous others effectually obstructing the command of the river from any single point. At the distance of about six hundred yards from the fort, to the south and east of it, is a circular valley, through which troops might be conducted completely under cover and secure from the guns of the fort. At the entrance of this valley, the enemy's troops landed in time of the late war, and under cover of a small mound a little in advance of it, commenced cannonading the old garrison (which occupied the highest part of the site of the present fort) with a three pounder, and soon compelled them to surrender. Immediately in rear of the place are the main river bluffs, at the distance of about one and a half miles from the fort. These are heights elevated four hundred and twenty feet above the site of the garrison, and overlook the whole of the Prairie du Chien. The site has been repeatedly subject to inundation, which is always to be apprehended when excessive floods prevail in the river. Indeed, the military features of the place generally are so faint and obscure, that they would hardly be perceptible, except by occupying several of the neighboring heights with castles and towers in order to protect an extensive work erected in the prairies below.

Saturday, 26.—Prairie du Chien is a handsome tract of low land, situated on the east side of the Mississippi, immediately above its confluence with the Ouisconsin. It is bounded on the east by the river bluffs, which stretch themselves along upon that side in nearly a straight direction, and occasionally intersected by ravines and valleys which afford easy communications with the hilly country situated back of the bluffs. The prairie is about ten miles in length, and from one to two and a half miles in breadth. In some parts it is handsomely variegated with swells and valleys that are secure from the inundations of the river; but in others, flat marshy lands, sloughs, and pools of water present themselves, which, although they add some embellishments to the scenery, serve to render the place unhealthy. Many parts of the prairie, which are sufficiently dry for culti- vation in the summer season, are subject to be overflowed whenever floods prevail in the river. The southerly part of the prairie is separated both from the Mississippi and the Ouisconsin by a large tract of marshy woodland extending along the shores of both rivers, and from half to one and a half miles in width. This tract in many places is cut by sloughs of moderate depth communica- ting with the main channels of the two rivers. The view of both rivers, from the prairie is generally ob- structed by the trees and shrubbery growing upon the marshy lands, as also by the numerous islands which both rivers imbosom, so that neither of them can be seen except in a very few instances. The bluffs on the west side of the Mississippi present themselves in gigantic forms immediately along the margin of the river, and extend up the river many miles, till they appear to be interrupted by those on the east. South of the Ouisconsin, the bluffs of the two rivers intercept each other, and form a stupendous promontory, between which and Pike's hill on the west, opens a broad vista, through which the two rivers flow, after having mingled their waters.

The village of Prairie du Chien, according to Pike, was first settled by the French in 1783. A man by the name of Giard, who died suddenly during my voyage up the Ouisconsin, is said to have been the first settler. He was of French and Indian extraction. Pike mentions two others, M. Antaya and Dubuque, who established themselves here at the same time with Giard. The ground occupied by these settlers was at a little distance below the present village. Exclusive of stores, workshops, and stables, the village at present contains only sixteen dwelling houses occupied by families. These are situated on a street parallel with the river, and about one half mile in length. In rear of the village, at the distance of three quarters of a mile, are four others. Two and a half miles above are five; and at the upper end of the prairie, five miles from the village, are four dwelling houses. Besides these, there are several houses situated upon different parts of the prairie, in all not exceeding seven or eight; so that the whole number of family dwellings, now occupied, does not exceed thirty-eight. The buildings are generally of logs, plastered with mud or clay; some of them comfortable habitations, but none of them exhibit any display of elegance or taste.

The inhabitants are principally of French and Indian extraction. There are very few of them that have not savage blood in their veins. If we compare the village and its inhabitants in their present state with what they were when Pike visited this part of the country, we shall find that instead of improving they have been degenerating. Their improvement has been checked by a diversion of the Indian into other channels, and their degeneracy accelerated not only by a consequent impoverishment of the inhabitants, but in addition to natural decay, their unconquerable slothfulness and want of enterprise.

About one mile back of the village is the Grand Farm, which is an extensive enclosure cultivated by the inhabitants in common. It is about six miles in length, and from a quarter to half a mile in width, surrounded by a fence on one side and the river bluffs on the other, and thus secured from the depredations of the cattle and horses that were at large upon the prairies. Upon this farm, corn, wheat, potatoes, etc., are cultivated to considerable advantage; and with proper care, no doubt, large crops of these articles, together with fruits of various kinds might be raised. They have never yet taken pains to seed the ground with any kind of grain except the summer wheat, which is never so productive as the fall or winter wheat. Rye, barley, oats, etc., would undoubtedly succeed well upon the farm.

The soil of the prairie is generally a silicious loam, containing more or less black mold, and is of various depths, from one to three feet. Below this is a bed of sand and small pebbles, extending probably to a considerable depth, and alternating with veins of clay and marl.

There are numerous antiquities discoverable upon various parts of the prairie, consisting of parapets, mounds, and cemeteries; relative to which the Indians have no traditions, and the oldest of them can give no account. They only suppose that the country was once inhabited by a race of white people like the present Americans, who have been completely exterminated by their forefathers. This supposition is grounded upon the circumstance of their having discovered human bones in the earth buried much deeper than the Indians are in the habit of burying their dead, and never accompanied by any implements of any kind, which the Indians have always been accustomed to bury with the body of their proprietor. Tomahawks of brass, and other implements, different from any the present Indians make use of, have also been found under the surface of the ground. They consider also the ancient fortifications another proof of the correctness of this opinion, as none of the Indians are in the habit of constructing works of a similar character, and indeed are unacquainted with the utility of them.

Mr. Brisbois, who has been for a long time a resident of Prairie du Chien, informed me that he saw the skeletons of eight persons, that were found in digging a cellar near his house, lying side by side. They were of gigantic size, measuring about eight feet from head to foot. He remarked that he took a leg bone of one of them and placed it by the side of his own leg in order to compare the length of the two. The bone of the skeleton extended six inches above his knee. None of these bones could be preserved as they crumbled to dust soon after they were exposed to the atmosphere.

The mounds probably were intended both as fortifications and cemeteries, as most of them, (perhaps all,) contain human bones, and at the same time appear to serve as flank defences to fortified lines. Whether the bones they contain are of the same character with those described by Mr. Brisbois I have not been able to ascertain.

The Prairie du Chien, or the Prairie of the Dog, derives its name from a family of Indians formerly known by the name of the Dog Indians, headed by a chief called the Dog. This family or band has become extinct. The Indians have some tradition concerning them. They say that a large party of Indians came down the Ouisconsin from Green Bay. That they attacked the family of the Dogs and massacred almost the whole of them, and returned again to Green Bay. That a few of the Dogs who had succeeded in making their escape to the woods, returned after their enemies had evacuated the Prairie, and re-established themselves in their former place of residence, and that these were the Indians inhabiting the Prairie at the time it was first settled by the French.

The inhabitants of Prairie du Chien have lately caused two small schools to be opened, in one of which the English language is taught and in the other the French. This augurs well of the future respectability of the place, if at the same time they would barter their slothful habits for those of industry.

Sunday, 27.—Having accomplished my business at the Prairie, I took leave of my friends, the officers of the

garrison, to whom I feel greatly indebted for the politeness and attention they have shown me, and particularly
to the commanding officer Capt. Duff'hey. The Sutler
also, Capt. Owens, evinced his friendship for me and the
cause in which I was engaged, by cheerfully supplying
me with funds without which I could not have prosecuted
my voyage with expedition or comfort. We re-embarked
at 10 o'clock A. M. to descend the Mississippi: My crew
now consisted of only five men, the same I took with
me from Belle Fontaine, with the exception of Sheffield.

Last evening Messrs. Gun and King arrived at the
Prairie from the Falls of St. Anthony. Whether they
accomplished the object of their trip, viz: to establish
their claim to the tract of country ceded by the Indians
to their grandfather Carver, I had no time to inquire,
but presume there is no ground for supposing they did,
as they before told me they could find but one Indian,
who had any knowledge of the transaction or was in the
least disposed to recognize the grant. That they do not
consider the cession obligatory upon them is very evident,
from there having ceded to the United States, through
the negotiations of Pike, two parcels of the same tract
specified in the grant in the favor of Carver.

Just before night we met the contractor Mr. Glen, on
his way to Prairie du Chien, with provisions for the
supply of the garrison at that place. He left St. Louis
on the 8th of June, seven days after I commenced my
voyage, and has been almost constantly engaged in
ascending the river ever since. When he left St. Louis
his boat was very heavily laden, having provisions on
board for the supply of Forts Edward, Armstrong, and

5

Crawford, for nine months. He found both rapids very difficult to pass, and has been frequently delayed by sand-bars. We spent some time with him and I supped on board his boat.

Monday, 28.—We floated last night till a strong head wind induced us to lay by. Had a shower of rain, accompanied by heavy thunder, about 2 A. M. Passed several canoes of Sauk Indians. The country on this part of the Mississippi which appeared beautiful, in a very high degree, when we ascended the river, seems to have lost half of its charms since we have visited the more noble scenery above.

Had strong head winds most of the day, so that our progress was very slow. Passed Dubuque's mines, in the morning, and arrived opposite the mouth of the River La Fievre, at evening, where we lay by to fish a little while, and afterwards commenced floating.

Tuesday, 29—At 10 o'clock last night there came on a violent thunder storm so that we were obliged to put into shore. It continued, with short intervals of abatement, through most of the night. The lightning appeared almost one continued blaze, and the thunder seemed to shake the earth to its centre, while the rain poured down in torrents. Our boat was in danger of filling from the vast quantity of rain that fell, so that we had frequent occasion to bail, in order to prevent her sinking. Started early this morning with a gentle breeze in our favor, which soon failed us, and was succeeded by a calm. The scenery we have passed to-day, although in many respects it is far less interesting than many views further up the river, yet has numberless beauties that give pleasure to the eye of the beholder, amongst which, precipices of red sand stone, fronting the river, are some of the most striking. They give to the bluffs a blushing appearance, which affords a very pleasing contrast when viewed in connection with the verdant attire in which they are clad. Passed Apin Prairie a little before night where we had another view of the beautiful scenery of this part of the river. But the idea that this beautiful tract has for ages unfolded its charms with none to admire, but unfeeling savages, instead of having delighted thousands that were capable of enjoying them, casts a gloom upon the scenery, which added to the solemn stillness that everywhere prevails in these solitary regions, robs the mind of half its pleasure.

Wednesday, 30.—The night was very fine and we floated about fifteen miles. This morning we passed Mer a Doge Prairie, before spoken of. Should there ever be occasion to station troops above the head of La Roche rapids, the first eligible position may be found on this prairie, as there are many positions, where a complete command of the river may be had, and troops stationed upon them, would not be exposed to the sudden annoyance of an enemy, as there would be no defile, through which he could approach without being discovered. Descended the La Roche rapids, without much difficulty, although the water was very low, and we had no one on board who was acquainted with the course of the channel.

Arrived at Fort Armstrong at about 12 o'clock.

Thursday, 31.—Spent the day in reconnoitering the country about the fort. Took observations for the latitude of Fort Armstrong, which I found to be 41° 32′ 33″ north.

Friday, August 1.—Having made the necessary surveys, I spent the day in plotting them and making a plan of the country adjacent to the site of Fort Armstrong. The island on which the fort is situated, is called Rock Island, from the circumstance of its being founded upon a rocky basis. It is situated immediately at the foot of La Roche rapids, is about three miles in length, and of various breadths, not exceeding one mile in the broadest part. At the lower extremity is the site of the fort, overlooking a large sheet of water, into which the Mississippi spreads immediately below, also extensive tracts of flat prairie situated on either side of the river within its valley. The valley is here about two miles wide, and is bounded on both sides by bluffs of gentle declivity, cut in many places by ravines of moderate depth. The elevation of the country back of the bluffs or hills is generally about one hundred feet above the water level, that of the prairies within the valley eight or ten, and that of the site of the fort, which is nearly at an intermediate distance between the bluffs, is thirty-two feet. The general course of the river past the island is west, southwest. The width of the north channel is six hundred and forty yards; that of the south two hundred and seventy-five yards; and the width of the whole river immediately below the island is fourteen hundred yards, which is the average width for about one mile below. Four miles below the island, Rock river comes in from the northeast. Upon the point of land situated between this river and the Missis-

sippi above their confluence, is an extensive level prairie
with a few scattering trees; this also is in full view from
the fort. To the south of the lower end of Rock Island
is another small island, annually subject to inundation,
though sufficiently elevated to admit of cultivation in
the summer season. It is separated from Rock Island
by a very narrow slough. It is ninety-seven yards wide
at its lower end, and tapers off to a point about eight
hundred yards farther up. Immediately opposite to the
fort on the south side of the river is a village of Fox
Indians, containing about thirty cabins, with two fires
each. The number of souls at this village is probably
about five hundred. On Rock river, two miles above its
mouth, and three across the point from Fort Armstrong,
is a Sack village, consisting of about one hundred cabins,
of two, three, and, in some instances, four fires each. It
is by far the largest Indian village situated in the neighborhood of the Mississippi between St. Louis and the
Falls of St. Anthony. The whole number of Indians at
this village amounts probably to between two and three
thousand. They can furnish eight or nine hundred warriors, all of them armed with rifles or fusees. The Indians of these two villages cultivate vast fields of corn,
which are situated partly in the low ground and extend
up the slopes of the bluffs. They have at present several
hundred acres under improvement in this way. The
soil of this part of the country is generally of an excellent quality, well adapted to the cultivation of corn, grain,
pulse, potatoes, flax, melons, etc. The natural growth
consists principally of oak, black walnut, cherry, and
hickory, affording excellent timber for building and other

purposes. Rock Island itself furnishes an abundance of these articles, being altogether woodland, except the lower end of it, which was cleared for the accommodation of the fort. The prairies yield an abundance of fine grass, and the country generally is well adapted for grazing. The country back of the river bluffs is rolling, and in some parts hilly, but is everywhere accessible by gentle ascents and declivities. The surface of Rock Island is undulating, inclining to hilly in the upper parts.

The site of Fort Armstrong, in a military point of view, is eligible, in many respects, and at the same time has fewer objections than any other position that can be found on the Mississippi, from St. Louis to the river St. Peter's. Its advantages are, a healthful situation, an effectual command of the river and of the neighboring prairies to the full extent of cannon shot range, security from the attack of an enemy armed with anything less than heavy artillery, timber and limestone of a good quality and in great abundance, rich grounds for gardens situated immediately above the garrison, a copious spring of fine water issuing from the cliffs a few rods above the site, etc. Its disadvantages are, a commanding rise elevated fifteen feet above the site, at the distance of two hundred yards in an easterly direction, which, if occupied by a suitable work, would be an important advantage, as it would give to the place a more extensive command; rising ground to the northeast, at a distance of half a mile; the river bluffs north-northwest, thirteen hundred, and those to the south sixteen hundred and fifty yards, from the site: the want of a convenient harbor for boats in low water. These disadvantages, compared with every other position, I have seen upon the river below the St. Peter's, are of little weight in point of objection. The advantages, in point of locality, are the facilities of communication either by land or water between this and other important parts of the country, which will be mentioned in their proper place, as also its central position in relation to the Indians.

Saturday, 2.—Took the dimensions of the fort and its buildings, and made a plan of them. The fort is situated immediately upon the lower extremity of Rock Island, at which place the shores are perpendicular cliffs of limestone thirty feet high. In some instances the cliffs project over their base, and even some parts of the fort overhang the water. The fort has two entire faces only, the other two sides being sufficiently fortified against an assault by the cliffs before mentioned. The east face commences immediately upon the top of the cliff, where there is a block house (No. 1) two stories high and twenty-one feet square. The front upon this side is two hundred and seventy-seven feet, including a block house (No. 2) at the northeast corner of the fort, twenty-six feet square. The north face forms a right angle with the east, and extends from block house No. 2 to the north channel of the river, where it is terminated by block house No. 3, of the same dimensions as No. 1, presenting a front on this side of two hundred and eighty-eight feet. Both faces are flanked by block house No. 2, the other block houses being placed in such a manner as to form a part of the front of the two faces. The block houses are all two stories high, their second stories being placed diagonally upon the first. No. 2 has also a basement story which is used as a store house. The faces are made up principally by the rear walls of the barracks and store house. They are about twenty feet high, and furnished with two rows of loopholes for muskets. The spaces between the buildings are fortified by walls of stone, about eight feet high, supporting a breast-work of timber five feet high. The buildings ranged along the faces contain seven rooms, twenty feet square, upon each side; eight of which are occupied as soldiers' quarters, three as hospitals, two as store-houses, and one as guard house. On the south and west sides detached from other parts of the works, are situated two other buildings sixty-four feet long and sixteen wide, containing four rooms each, designed for officers' quarters. In the southwest corner is a two story building with low wings, designed as quarters for the commanding officer, and offices for the use of the garrison. The body of the building is furnished with piazzas on both sides, and the whole combines a degree of taste and elegance worthy of imitation at all other military posts in this part of the country.

The works are constructed principally of square timber, the lower part of the block houses, including lower embrasures of stone. The magazine also is of stone, seven by ten feet in the clear, its walls four feet in thickness. Besides these there are a few other buildings outside of the garrison, viz., a smith's shop, suttler's and contractor's stores, a stable, etc.

The plan of defence is at present incomplete, there being three points where an enemy might approach the garrison completely under cover from the works. The first is at the lower point of the island directly under the brow of the cliffs which stretch along that extremity in nearly a straight direction, one hundred and fifty yards from the fort, eastwardly. The second is the rise before mentioned, eastward of the fort, beyond which there is a gentle declivity to the water's edge through an expanding valley. The third is a kind of bay situated just above a prominent part of the island, upon the north side, by which the fire from the fort into the bay would be obstructed. In this bay also is situated the spring before described, so that a command of this place is the more desirable on that account.

To remedy the first defect, a water battery may be constructed, immediately at the point of the island, which will give a far more complete command of the river below than the present works designed for that purpose, and at the same time its east face would completely flank the cliffs in that direction. To obviate the second and third defects, the block houses, No. 1 and No. 3, might be removed, one on the commanding rise to the east, and the other on the eminence to the north of the garrison. These block houses in their present situation have no command that they would not have after being removed to the places proposed; and where they now stand a breast work would be a far better substitute. No. 3, particularly, is badly situated; it projects considerably over the water and is partly supported by wooden props, so that should the river continue to undermine the bank, there would be great danger of its being precipitated into the water.

Having completed my plans, we re-embarked at 3 P. M. to descend the river. Passed Rock River four miles below the Fort. This river in high water is navigable about three hundred miles to what are called the Four Lakes, but in its present stage, which is the usual height at this season of the year, it is with great difficulty that a canoe can ascend it even three or four miles. There are numerous rapids which make their appearance in various parts of the river when the water is low, but at other times there are none perceptible throughout the above mentioned distance. The Indians residing upon this river, beside the Sack village before mentioned, are principally Winnebagoes, with some few of the Ioways and Fol avoins, most of whom have their residence in the neighborhood of the Four Lakes. Between the head waters of Rock River and those of Lake Michigan, is a portage of moderate extent through which some trade is carried on with the Indians.

At evening, when we had got twenty miles from the Fort, I discovered that I had left my sextant, which made it necessary for us to encamp for the night in order to send a man back for it in the morning, as it would be impossible for me to take observations for the latitude without it.

Sunday, 3.—Dispatched a man for the sextant early this morning, with orders to return to Fort Edwards, either in the contractor's boat which is daily expected down, or in the express boat which must come in a few days to Fort Edwards. Started a little after sunrise. The wind strong ahead all day. Encamped at the east side at the Red Banks, the wind being too strong to admit of floating.

Monday, 4.—Started at an early hour. Went on shore in the afternoon to revisit the ruins of Fort Madison. There was nothing but old chimneys left standing, and a covert way leading from the main garrison to an elevated ground in the rear, upon which there was some kind of an outwork. The covert way was fortified with palisades only. There were a number of fruit trees also standing upon the ground formerly occupied as a garden, amongst which were the peach, the nectarine and the apple tree.

Descended the Rapids De Moin a little before sunset, but as none of us was acquainted with the channel, and the water very low, we ran foul of rocks a number of times, which occasioned a leak in our boat, so that we had to keep a man constantly bailing, to prevent her filling with water. Arrived at Fort Edwards about dark, the men very much fatigued with rowing and getting the boat across the rapids.

Tuesday, 5.—Gave the men an opportunity to rest themselves, while I took an excursion on foot about the place.

Wednesday, 6.—Concluded to ascend the rapids again, and take a short tour in the country above. In this excursion I was joined by Dr. Lane and Capt. Calhoun. Having a fair wind, we set sail about 11 A. M. but after passing half way up the rapids, the wind failed us, and we had recourse to rowing. Ascended within four miles of the head of the rapids, and encamped for the night.

Thursday, 7.—Started early and arrived at the head of the Rapids, at Ewing's plantation, (formerly known by the name of the United States' Agricultural Establishment) at half past 8 o'clock. Here we breakfasted and as the wind was strong ahead, concluded to leave the boat and travel on foot further up. The two gentlemen before mentioned, myself and two soldiers, made up the party. We accoutered ourselves with rifles, ammunition and two days' supply of provisions, having a pack horse which was sent up for the purpose, to convey our baggage. We pursued the course of the river, on the east side, about twenty miles, to a prairie a little above Fort Madison. We then turned to the right, and travelled due east about six miles, when we encamped for the night near a small creek running north. Near the place of our encampment observed a tree marked by the surveyors as follows, R. 7 N. T. 7 W. S. 9, being the corner bound, of one of the towns recently surveyed in this part of the country. The country in a direction due east from the river, in this place, is considerably broken, being interrupted by numerous water courses and ravines. But the season being unusually dry few of them contained any water at the time we were there.

Friday, 8.—Started about sunrise and travelled about S. W., and came upon an extensive prairie, about two miles from the place of our encampment. We had not proceeded far when we struck upon an Indian trail, leading nearly in the direction we contemplated to take, viz. W. S. W. We accordingly pursued it fifteen miles, and arrived at our boat about 12 o'clock. The whole of this distance lay through an extensive prairie, cutting off but a very small fraction of it. This vast tract of level country occupies most of the space included between the Mississippi and Illinois, commencing at Rock River on the former, and Fox River on the latter, and extending downward nearly to the junction of the two.

After dining we commenced descending the river again. Passed the Rapids with less difficulty than before. Killed a pelican. Stopped awhile at the foot of the rapids to examine the stratifications which we found of a similar character with those generally along the Mississippi. While we were engaged in this examination one of the men found a hive of bees, which they soon took and found in it about two gallons of honey. Arrived at the garrison about 5 P. M.

Saturday, 9.—Spent the day in sketching the country about Fort Edwards, the garrison, etc. Fort Edwards is situated on the east side of the Mississippi three miles below the foot of De Moyen Rapids. The Mississippi at this place is about one thousand four hundred yards wide ; the main channel is on the west side ; the passage on the east, particularly in low water, is obstructed by sand-bars. Directly opposite to the Fort are two islands, dividing the De Moyen, which comes in on the west at this place, into three mouths. About one mile above the Fort, on the same side of the river, is an island of considerable extent. The bluffs at this place, approach immediately to the water's edge, on the east, but on the west are separated from the river by an extensive tract of bottom land, covered with a fine growth of cottonwood, sycamore, and black walnut. The site of the Fort is elevated one hundred feet above low water mark. Its distance horizontally from the river is about sixty yards. At the distance of half a mile from the Fort, in a S. W. direction, is the site of Cantonment Davis, which has been abandoned since the erection of Fort Edwards. The country situated between the two sites is cut by deep ravines, which have meandering courses and approach in some places within musket shot range from both sites. To the N. E. of Fort Edwards is a commanding height at the distance of six hundred yards, separated from the site of the Fort by a broad ravine, and elevated fifty feet above it, or one hundred and fifty feet above the river. The country adjacent to the Fort to the eastward and N. E. is considerably broken and abounds in ravines. Southeastwardly of the Fort the country has nearly the same level as the site on which it is built. The ground generally in the neighborbood is covered with a scattering growth of hickory, oak, and walnut; the hill to the N. E. however is covered with deep woods. In regard to the military character of the place, many objections present themselves. 1st. No effectual command of either river can be had, not only on account of the great width of the Mississippi, but also, a slough leading to the west of the river from which it is separated by an island about one mile wide, and communicating with the Mississippi at the distance of of one mile below, and one and one-half miles above, the site of the garrison. Through this slough the De Moyen discharges its waters and boats may pass with facility in time of high water. 2d. The ravine before mentioned would facilitate the approach of an enemy to within a musket shot range of the garrison, completely under cover from its fire. 3rd. The commanding height to the N. E. would render the position untenable though ever so strongly fortified, provided an enemy should

occupy it with ordnance of moderate calibre. 4th. From
the situation of the place no important end can be answered by keeping up a garrison at it, except perhaps in
time of actual warfare with the Indians. The only
object that presents itself in this point of view, is its
proximity to the rapids above, and the protection that
might be afforded by the garrison to supplies, stores,
etc., in their passage up the rapids. But in this respect
no advantage would be derived from a garrison at this
place more than at any other upon the river, provided
transports of every kind are conveyed up and down the
river in their proper season, viz., from the 1st of April to
the middle of June, when there is always a sufficient
depth of water to pass the rapids, with a current but
little more accelerated than is to be met with in other
parts of the river.

The distance from this place to Fort Clark on the
Illinois is about seventy-five miles, across a level tract
of prairie country, and about one hundred and twenty
to Fort Osage on the Missouri, across a level country,
principally prairie. In the neighborhood of rivers
and creeks, in this direction, the country is somewhat
broken.

Fort Edwards is a palisade work constructed entirely
of square timber. It is intended to contain two block
houses, situated in the alternate angles of the Fort; a
magazine of stone; barracks for the accommodation of
one company of soldiers; officers' quarters; hospital;
store-rooms, etc.; all to be constructed in a simple but
neat style, but on a scale too contracted for comfortable
accommodations. The works are in such a state of for-

wardness that they will probably be nearly completed this season. The magazine is still to be built, as are also the officers' quarters, hospital, etc. They have been wholly executed by the soldiery stationed there since June, 1816.

Sunday, 10.—Had to finish my plans of Fort Edwards and the adjacent country, and make preparations for resuming my voyage. I yesterday took an observation for the latitude of the place, and found the meridian altitude of the sun's lower limb to be 65° 12' 46".

Monday, 11.—Started at half-past 6 A. M. in company with Dr. Lane, to ascend the river De Moyen a few miles. We entered at its lowermost mouth, passed the middle, which at this time had no water passing through it, and ascended about two miles to the uppermost, through which is the principal discharge of the De Moyen in low water. We ascended the river about three miles higher, where the channel was completely obstructed by sand bars, affording not even a sufficiency of water for the navigation of the smallest canoes. The water in the river, however, was at this time unusually low. Nevertheless, there is seldom a sufficiency of water at this season of the year to admit boats to ascend very far. In the spring of the year deep floods usually prevail in the river, which render it navigable for Mackinaw boats one hundred and sixty or two hundred miles.

The river is about one hundred and twenty yards wide near its confluence with the Mississippi. Its upper mouth affords a considerable depth of water in all stages, but the channel is narrow and crooked, and almost blocked up in many places by drift wood, snags, and sawyers. The passage by the lower mouths is much broader, but obstructed in many places by sand bars that are impassable in low water. The principal part of the Ioway Indians reside up this river, at the distance of about one hundred and twenty miles from its mouth.

Observed many fragments of coal, apparently of a good quality, scattered upon the sand bars in this river.

Returned about twelve. Dined and took my leave of Dr. Lane, and Captain Ramsay, commanding officer of the garrison. To Dr. Lane in particular I feel much indebted for his politeness and attention. Captain Calhoun was about to take his departure, on a visit to his friends, and I invited him to take a passage to Belle Fontaine in my boat, with which he complied. We started at 2 P. M., the wind ahead. Met several canoes of Indians.

Tuesday, 12.—Floated till one at night, when we were compelled to lay by on account of an unfavorable wind accompanied with rain. Started again at sunrise. A favorable wind sprang up at 1 P. M., and we were able to sail the rest of the day.

Wednesday, 13—Floated all night, and arrived at Burr's Tavern early in the morning. Were able to sail most of the day moderately. Arrived at Little Cape Gris about dark, and encamped.

Thursday, 14.—Captain Calhoun, myself, and one of the men, took an excursion across the country this morning, and went in sight of the shores of the Illinois. Independent of the bluffs, there is a ridge of land elevated about eighteen feet above the water level, extending from the Mississippi to the Illinois. The distance be-

6

tween the two rivers along this ridge is about four and a
half miles. The bluffs of the two rivers meet each other
at the distance of about one mile in rear of the ridge,
being a succession of knobs forming an extensive curve
between the two rivers. The soil is of a good quality,
inclining to sandy in some places. Growth principally
oak, hickory, black and white walnut, sycamore, cottonwood, persimmon, and pawpaw. Upon the point below
the ridge is a large prairie extending to the Illinois. There
are five settlements at this place, including two immediately upon the Mississippi at Little Cape Gris. Started
at half-past eight. Weather rainy. Called at Portage
de Sioux. Arrived at the mouth of the Missouri about
6 P. M., and ascended it half a mile, where we encamped
for the night.

Friday, 15.—Arrived at Belle Fontaine at nine in the
morning, all in good health. Three of my men had experienced a short illness of one day each, having been
attacked with the fever and ague. But by a seasonable
application of remedies neither of them had a return of
the chill. The mode of treatment I adopted towards
them was to administer a cathartic of calomel and jalap
soon after the shake or chill was off, and the next day,
sometime before the return of the fever was expected,
require the patient to take freely of wine and bark,
which invariably had the desired effect.

The time occupied in the voyage was seventy-six
days.

Latitude in the Mississippi, 1½ miles above the mouth of the St. Peter's, 45° 7′ 8″.

Latitude at Prairie du Chien, 43° 7′; by a lunar observation, 43° 6′ 14″.

Fort Armstrong, Rock Island, 41° 27′ 29″.

At Fort Edwards, De Moyen, 40° 22′ 19″.

At the Wisconsin Portage, 44°.

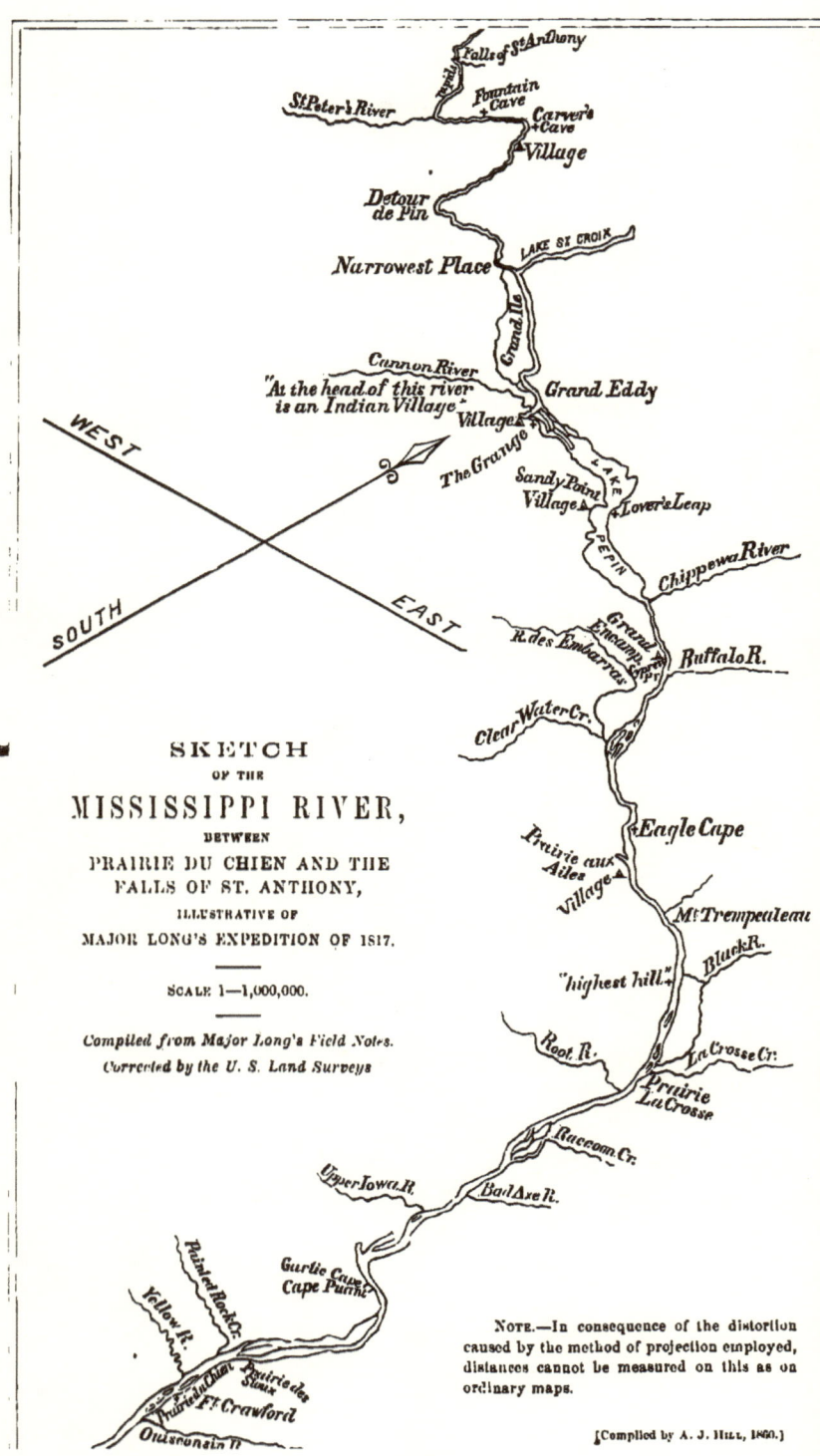

SKETCH
OF THE
MISSISSIPPI RIVER,
BETWEEN
PRAIRIE DU CHIEN AND THE
FALLS OF ST. ANTHONY,
ILLUSTRATIVE OF
MAJOR LONG'S EXPEDITION OF 1817.

SCALE 1—1,000,000.

Compiled from Major Long's Field Notes.
Corrected by the U. S. Land Surveys

NOTE.—In consequence of the distortion
caused by the method of projection employed,
distances cannot be measured on this as on
ordinary maps.

[Compiled by A. J. HILL, 1860.]

APPENDIX.

AFTER the Journal had been printed, A. J. Hill, Esq., an accurate and accomplished Civil Engineer, forwarded a compiled itinerancy of Major Long's tour, and a map illustrative of the same. It is with great pleasure that we append the correspondence, map and annotations of Mr. Hill.

E. D. N.

Saint Paul, October 15, 1860.

SAINT PAUL, MINNESOTA.
September 29, 1860.

REV. E. D. NEILL,
Sec. Minnesota Historical Society,

DEAR SIR :—I herewith have the pleasure to enclose for your use, a compiled intinerary of Major Long's tour of 1817, and a diagram to illustrate the same; and trust they will be received in proper time. The delay in the transmission of these papers arose from the fact of my having for the last five days been busily engaged in writing for Col. Robertson. Enclosed is a memorandum containing a few topographical annotations some of which may be suggestive if not literally used

A few words are necessary as to the map. After considerable thought, I concluded that an ordinarily projected map of the river would be of very little ornament or use to the book, from the necessarily small scale required to comprise the tract of country in question within a page of the size of your history, and that the system of projection technically called "isometrical"—which allows of considerable foreshortening— might be employed to advantage, as not so much a *map* as a sketch or diagram, ("conspectes") is needed for such a work. Should you conclude to have it engraved, I would respectfully suggest that it may be done so in its integrity and without any *modernization* or additions as respects names or town-sites, my idea being to make only such a sketch as might have been made by Major Long himself at the time, except that I have corrected his meanderings by the United States Land Surveys. If engraved I will gladly inspect a proof, if sent (2 copies) to me at Red Wing, and return promptly with remarks.

On the sheet of "errata" furnished was one altered number which I could not at the time find for your inspection, so I have *traced* it on the corner of the enclosed diagram; it most probably is "50," if necessary a foot note might speak of its ambiguity.

Next Monday I leave St. Paul for Red Wing.

I remain, Sir, very respectfully

Your obedient servant,

ALFRED J. HILL.

TOPOGRAPHICAL ANNOTATIONS, MAJOR LONG, 1817.

PREPARED BY A. J. HILL, CIVIL ENGINEER.

The "highest hill" is situated at the present village of Richmond in Winona County; its height above the level of the water was ascertained by Nicollet to be 531 feet.

Prarie Aux Ailes village, on the site of the present Winona.

Grand Encampment on Cypress Prairie, the present Tepeeotah.

In ascending the river immediately alone, Lake Pepin, Long kept to the middle and northern channels, which accounts for his not mentioning Barn Bluff here.

"Narrowest place in the river," the present Hastings.

Detour de Pin, now Pine Bend.

Petit Corbeau's village, afterwards Pig's Eye.

Height of Barn Bluff according to Nicollet above water 322 feet. Owen's "about 350." Red Wing City Survey (1859) "345½ feet above the level of the low water."

Table of distances on the Mississippi River from Prairie du Chien (Fort Crawford) to the Falls of Saint Anthony.

NAMES OF PLACES.	Estimated by Maj. Long in 1817. (Miles.)		According to the U. S. Land Surveys. (Miles.)	
	Intermediate.	Total.	Intermediate.	Total.
From Fort Crawford to the mouth of the Upper Iowa River,	43	43	34½	34½
" mouth of Upper Iowa River to mouth of Bad Axe River,	5½	48½	4½	39
" mouth of Bad Axe River to mouth of Raccoon Creek,	15	63½	9	48
" mouth of Raccoon Creek to mouth of Root River,	13	76½	9	57
" mouth of Root River to mouth of La Crosse Creek,	6½	83	4	61
" mouth of La Crosse Creek to lower mouth of Black River,	1½	84½	1	62
" lower mouth of Black River to upper mouth of Black River,	14	98½	12	74
" upper mouth of Black River to Trempealean Mountain,	8	106½	6	80
" Trempealeau Mountain to Prairie aux Ailes Village,	9	115½	7	87
" Prairie aux Ailes Village to Eagle Cape,	7	122½	5½	92½
" Eagle Cape to mouths of Embarras and Clear Water Rivers, (united,)	14	136½	10	102½
" mouth of Embarras, &c., Rivers to mouth of Buffalo River,	12	148½	10	112½
" mouth of Buffalo River to Grand Encamp.,	4	152½	3	115½
" Grand Encampment to mouth of Chippewa River,	7	159½	7	122½
" mouth of Chippewa River to outlet of Lake Pepin,	1½	161	1	123½
" outlet of Lake Pepin to Lovers' Leap,	12	173	11½	135
" Lovers' Leap to Indian Encampment on Sandy Point on left,	1	174	1	136
" Sandy Point to inlet of Lake, middle channel,	9	183	9	145
" inlet of Lake to *opposite* mouth of Cannon River,	5½	188½	5½	150½
" opposite mouth of Cannon River to the "Grand Eddy,"	1½	190	1½	152
" the Grand Eddy to the mouth of Lake St. Croix,	18	208	16½	168½
" mouth of Lake St. Croix to the "narrowest place in the river,"	6½	214½	2½	171
" "narrowest place" to Detour de Pin (Pine Turn,)	12½	227	10	181
" Detour de Pin to village of Petit Corbeau,	16½	243½	11¾	192¾
" Village of Petit Corbeau to Carver's Cave,	2	245½	2	194¾
" Carver's Cave to Fountain Cave,	5	250½	4	198¾
" Fountain Cave to mouth of St. Peter's River,	5	255½	3	201¾
" mouth of St. Peter's River to commencement of rapids,	2	257½	1½	203¼
" commencement of rapids to mouth of creek on right hand,	7½	265	6	209¼
" mouth of creek to the foot of the Falls of St. Anthony,	1	266	¾	210

www.ingramcontent.com/pod-product-compliance
Lightning Source LLC
Chambersburg PA
CBHW032354020726
47499CB00008B/2739